HORROR

HOR

R O R

CONTENTS

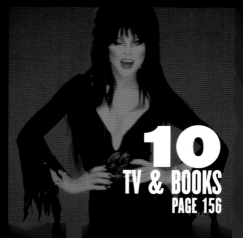

We love horror. We are endlessly entertained by it. But why do we love to be scared?

Countless theories and literally hundreds of scientific treatises have attempted to explain this phenomenon. Is it the dopamine that fear releases into the brain? The adrenaline? The enjoyment of having an intense emotional reaction? The pleasure of being scared, and then getting satisfaction later when there's a moment of relief? The communal experience of seeing a scary movie with an audience that's just as jumpy as you are? Depending on whose work you read, it's any of those, or maybe it's a combination, or maybe it's something else entirely.

Ultimately, does science or psychology really matter? The horror genre has never been more popular. Movies with small budgets make hundreds of millions of dollars, because people are lining up to see them— or staying home to stream them. TV networks dedicate more programming hours to horror than ever before. Hundreds of movies and TV shows, some of them new originals, are available 24/7 on a streaming horror-video service called Shudder. Podcasts put frightening audio fiction at your fingertips all day long. Video games put players right into the horror. Bookstores, both brick-and-mortar and online, have a hard time keeping scary novels in stock.

In short, people can't get enough horror these days. And neither can we. So, over the following pages, we'll look at various forms of the genre: their history, their popularity, why they're so effective, and what makes people love them so. We'll zero in on vampires, zombies, mummies, werewolves, aliens, creeps, creatures, witches, demons, slashers and the supernatural. The movies, the TV, the books, the folklore, the humor—we're looking at it all. We'll go back centuries, and sometimes even millennia, to explore the incredible history of the genre: its origins, its evolution and where it is today.

Yes, we're doing a deep dive into what makes horror so horrendously horrific, so strap yourself onto the slab and get ready. There are some serious scares ahead!

—*Neil Turitz and Barak Zimmerman*

HELLO, HORROR

DRACULA, 1979

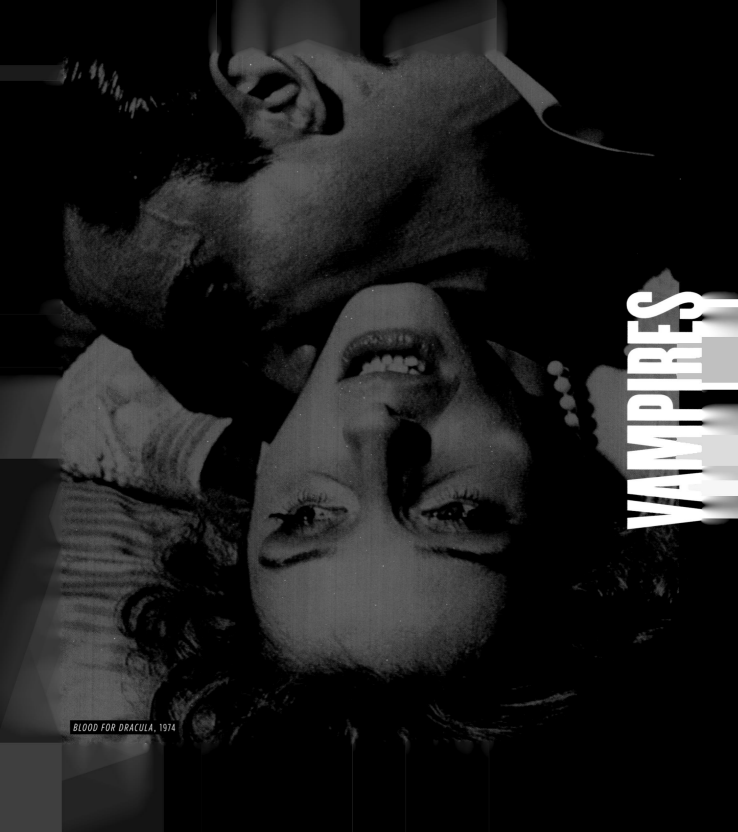

VAMPIRES

BLOOD FOR DRACULA, 1974

LONG IN THE TOOTH

THEY'RE SEXY. THEY'RE ANCIENT. THEY'RE DEAD—AND STILL THEY VANT TO SUCK YOUR BLOOD. A BRIEF HISTORY OF DRACULA AND A HOST OF OTHER VAMPIRES.

What is it about Dracula that fascinates us so deeply? There's the sex factor, of course: the seduction. Vampires go for blood, often from the neck, and there's something romantic, steamy, even sensual about that.

But there's another thing about vampires that is just as appealing: immortality. Living forever can seem like a good deal, even if that life—or afterlife—can be lived only at night. Maybe that's part of the appeal, too. To say nothing of the shape-shifting: Dracula was the original bat man.

Ever since Bram Stoker published *Dracula* in 1897, that name and the word "vampire" have been nearly synonymous. Bloodsuckers had been part of folklore for more than 600 years, but Count Dracula was the first stylish, courtly incarnation—the first monster to capture the popular imagination in an embrace both compelling and horrifying.

But first, a little history. The first recorded mentions of vampires are found in two 12th-century texts from England. Then, a few hundred years later, along came Vlad the Impaler.

Born around 1428, Vlad Tepes ruled Wallachia three times in the mid-1400s. When he wasn't making life miserable for his subjects, he lived in exile in nearby Transylvania. He enjoyed killing prisoners and criminals by impaling them alive on stakes, even treating the spectacle as dinner theater. Today, he remains one of the nastiest, bloodthirstiest tyrants ever.

And his name lives in infamy. "Dracula" is based on his father's name, Dracul, after the Order of the Dracul, or Dragon. Thanks to Vlad's cruelty, Dracula became a

As Frances Dade's Lucy slumbers, Bela Lugosi's Count closes in for the suck in 1931's *Dracula*.

"THERE ARE FAR WORSE THINGS AWAITING MAN THAN DEATH."

—Dracula to Mina Seward, in the 1931 film

11

Vlad Tepes, aka
Vlad the Impaler,
Prince of
Wallachia

"I HAVE KILLED PEASANTS, MEN AND WOMEN, OLD AND YOUNG... WHERE THE DANUBE FLOWS INTO THE SEA."

—Vlad Tepes, in a 1462 letter to a military ally

name that was synonymous with "the devil."

Centuries after Vlad's assassination in 1477, vampire frenzies swept Central Europe and Russia in the 1700s. In the throes of such madness, officials would visit afflicted towns to dig up corpses, check them for fresh blood and stake them. Think: Salem witch trials level of hysteria.

But why? Well, medicine was fairly primitive, and doctors often mistook a coma for death. If a person regained consciousness in an open coffin, they seemed to be "undead"—which they in fact were. They were alive. But still, it shook people up.

Also, the Greek Orthodox Church said that the bodies of heretics would not decompose after death. The Catholic Church said the same of saints' bodies. Both denominations were popular in Central Europe, making it fertile ground for legends and hysteria to bloom.

And from madness came art: Within a few decades, vampires would go on to become popular in poems, operas and plays.

Lord Byron, for instance, claimed in his 1813 poem "The Giaour" to have been visited by a vampire. He inspired John Polidori to write the novel *The Vampyre* just three years later. Alexandre Dumas of *Three Musketeers* fame also

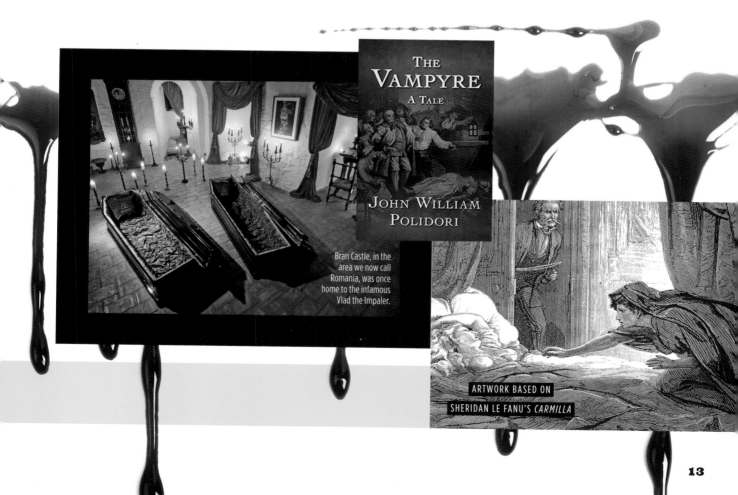

THE VAMPYRE
A TALE

JOHN WILLIAM POLIDORI

Bran Castle, in the area we now call Romania, was once home to the infamous Vlad the Impaler.

ARTWORK BASED ON SHERIDAN LE FANU'S *CARMILLA*

wrote a play entitled *Le Vampire*, which opened in Paris in 1851. In 1873, Sheridan Le Fanu introduced the first female vampire in English literature in his book *Carmilla*. The title character appears in the form of a beautiful, mysterious young woman who takes shelter with an isolated family and dotes on their teenage daughter. Meanwhile, neighboring women start to sicken and die. Eventually, she is revealed as an ancestor of the family—but they thought she'd died 150 years earlier. By the last page, she is laid to her eternal rest.

Each of these works likely influenced Stoker's masterpiece, which would soon launch vampires—Dracula, especially— back into the mainstream. The story of how Stoker created such a work is itself fascinating. A sickly child, young Bram enjoyed his father's library and the gruesome tales his mother told. He began writing ghost stories even as a boy, declaring that his efforts would someday make him famous. He went on to publish reviews, articles and a few melodramatic books, with little success. As he neared age 50, his dreams of fame seemed fairly remote.

Then Stoker met the Hungarian adventurer Arminius Vámbéry, who told him about the vampire stories of Eastern Europe. Stoker had never been to Transylvania, but shortly after that meeting, he began to research the region.

As the vampire Barnabas Collins, Jonathan Frid brought terror to daytime TV on the original *Dark Shadows*.

MAX SCHRECK,
IN *NOSFERATU*
1922

KLAUS KINSKI,
IN *NOSFERATU*
THE VAMPYRE
1979

FRANK LANGELLA,
IN *DRACULA*
1979

15

Ben Cross, as
Barnabas Collins,
on the short-lived
1991 TV remake of
Dark Shadows.

BELA LUGOSI, IN *DRACULA*
1931

WILLIAM MARSHALL, IN *BLACULA*
1972

HOW TO KILL IT

1. DRIVE A WOODEN STAKE THROUGH THE HEART.

2. EXPOSE VAMPIRE TO SUNLIGHT. (Warning: Old-school vampires will burn up, but modern variations may be immune.)

He read books about the history of Wallachia and Moldavia and about the Carpathian countryside, its castles and customs.

How much he drew on the Transylvanian legends of Vlad Tepes and Hungarian noblewoman Elizabeth Báthory (see "The Countess Drank Blood," p. 19) is up for debate. But when the book was published in 1897, its combination of sex and scares hit a nerve in repressed Victorian society. It was popular from the start and has never been out of print, but the novel's fame really exploded when it spawned a hit play—and then came the movies.

The most memorable of the early horror silent movies is

F. W. Murnau's *Nosferatu*, a highly atmospheric 1922 German Expressionist film that combined Stoker's storyline with a more traditional demonic look. Murnau and company changed the names (Dracula became Orlock) and details (London became Bremen) to avoid paying royalties. Stoker's widow sued the film company and shut it down, ordering all prints destroyed. Luckily, a few survived, and the film has become an influential classic.

Perhaps the most influential vampire film of all time, however, is director Tod Browning's *Dracula*. Released by Universal in 1931, it made a movie star of Bela Lugosi and introduced horror to

the mainstream. Soon after would come *Frankenstein*, *The Bride of Frankenstein*, *The Mummy*, *The Invisible Man* and many others.

Even though Lugosi didn't fit Stoker's description of the count, he became the world's best-known Dracula. He'd starred in the Broadway play that kicked off Dracula-mania in the mid-1920s, but still had to lobby hard to win the film part. His heavily accented delivery of such famous lines as "I bid you velcome," "Listen to them—children of the night," and "I never drink...wine" are synonymous with the character, as are his slow, stately movements. Actor David Manners, who played Jonathan Harker, said Lugosi would stand before a long mirror on the set and say, "I am Dracula" over and over. (Funny, because vampires don't appear in mirrors.)

Nearly lost to history was the Spanish version. Studios often shot foreign-language versions at night to get more use out of the sets, so every night, a different cast and crew came in and shot *Drácula*. The movie was rediscovered and restored in the 1970s. Many fans now say it's a better film than Browning's, with superior acting, pacing and camera work.

The success of *Dracula* led Universal to make sequels and spinoffs through the 1930s and 1940s, with titles like *Mark of the Vampire*, *Dracula's Daughter* and *Son of Dracula*. The count also appeared, with diminishing returns, in so-called "monster rallies"—all-star horrorfests like *House of Frankenstein* (1944) and *House of Dracula* (1945). Universal eventually closed the coffin and put the count to rest.

In 1958, Britain's Hammer Studios made the first of two Dracula movies starring British thespian Christopher Lee, who truly looked the part. *Horror of Dracula* updated the character (in color!). It was followed eight years later by a sequel, *Dracula: Prince of Darkness*; six years after that came *Dracula A.D. 1972*, which finds the count in swinging London.

Meanwhile, from 1966 to 1971, ABC aired a weekday soap opera

CAMPAIGN BOO...
YOU WON'T DARE BELIEVE - WHAT YOUR EY...
Lionel BARRYMORE in
MARK OF THE VAMPIRE
Elizabeth with Béla ALLAN · LUGOSI
Lionel Jean ATWILL · HERSHOLT
Tod Browning's *Production*

CHRISTOPHER LEE, IN *HORROR OF DRACULA*
1958

LON CHANEY JR. AND GEORGE IRVING, IN *SON OF DRACULA*
1943

Bloodthirsty
Elizabeth
Báthory:
She put the
hunger
in Hungary.

THE COUNTESS DRANK BLOOD

Elizabeth Báthory (1560–1614) was a Hungarian noblewoman, born in Transylvania to a friend of the king who then married a count. Believing that the blood of young women would keep her young and her skin pale, she employed a staff of servants to lure, entrap and then "milk" young women of their blood. Some victims were bled for days; others died more swiftly. Báthory's staff set up her torture chamber everywhere she went.

Her status helped to keep the law at bay, even as rumors spread and maidens continued to vanish. It's estimated that she and her staff killed 600 or so women in 15 years, before they were caught and sentenced to death. Even then, her nobility protected her. Instead of death, she received life imprisonment in her castle, where she was bricked up for three years before she died. Her story has inspired dozens of films.

called *Dark Shadows*, which saw vampire Barnabas Collins lead a cast of ghosts, werewolves, zombies, witches and more. (Johnny Depp played Collins in an ill-fated 2012 movie version.)

The year 1972 brought the blaxploitation epic *Blacula*; next came *Scream, Blacula, Scream* a year later. The gates were open: *Andy Warhol's Blood for Dracula* (1974) was a campy, sexy comedy; *Dracula's Dog* (1977) was as silly as it sounds; and *Love at First Bite* (1979) was a rom-com, set in Manhattan!

In 1977, though, Frank Langella restored some dignity to the count when he starred on Broadway in *Dracula*, a big-budget remake of the 1927 play, with sets by goth-y illustrator Edward Gorey. In 1979, he starred in a film adaptation. The last big-budget retelling was

JOHNNY DEPP, IN *DARK SHADOWS* 2012

He couldn't live without a virgin's blood.....

ANDY WARHOL'S BLOOD FOR DRACULA

...So a virgin had to die!

ANN MAGNUSON AND DAVID BOWIE, IN *THE HUNGER* 1983

George Hamilton, star of the spoofy *Love at First Bite*, is shown here in the poster art with Susan Saint James, Arte Johnson (bottom left) and Richard Benjamin.

Fright Night brought vampires to the suburbs, with Roddy McDowall baring his fangs.

LUKE PERRY AND KRISTY SWANSON, IN *BUFFY THE VAMPIRE SLAYER*
1992

TOM CRUISE AND INDRA OVÉ, IN *INTERVIEW WITH THE VAMPIRE*
1994

Francis Ford Coppola's *Bram Stoker's Dracula*, which starred Gary Oldman and won three technical Oscars in 1992.

But who's counting? Dracula aside, vampires really make up a many-splendored genre. In 1983, Catherine Deneuve, David Bowie and Susan Sarandon starred in *The Hunger,* a stylish love story. In 1985, the teen horror comedy *Fright Night* brought vampirism to suburbia, while the 1987 cult film *The Lost Boys* starred a young Kiefer Sutherland. That same year, director Kathryn Bigelow's landmark *Near Dark* portrayed bloodsuckers as a roving road gang in the American Southwest. Nine years later, Quentin Tarantino wrote and co-starred with George Clooney in *From Dusk Till Dawn,* in which a horde of vampires at a truck stop terrorizes two crooks on the lam.

Of course, the 1992 movie *Buffy the Vampire Slayer* became a wildly popular WB/UPN TV show of the same name, which ran from 1997 to 2003 and inspired a spinoff (*Angel*), a comic book...and a shocking number of academic papers.

One of the first movies to feature a Marvel Comics character was 1998's *Blade,* which starred Wesley Snipes as a half-man/half-vampire hunter of...vampires. It led to two sequels. On The CW, *The Vampire Diaries*—inspired by L. J. Smith's book series of the same name—ran for eight seasons, ending in 2017.

Its spinoff, *The Originals,* ran until 2018.

These are just some of the vampires who have darkened our screens over the years. Meanwhile, a whole genre of literature has arisen from this restless grave. Smith, Stephen King, Justin Cronin and Laurell K. Hamilton, to name a few, have written books that feature vampires. But we can thank three women for the top modern vampires. Each relies on elements of historical lore but carves out a very distinct world.

In 1976, Anne Rice published *Interview With the Vampire,* the first of her wildly popular Lestat novels. (It became a 1994 movie starring Tom Cruise, Brad Pitt and Kirsten Dunst.) Her *Vampire Chronicles* series is a dozen books— or more, depending on which of her vampire books you count.

In 2001, Charlaine Harris started the *Dead Until Dark* novels about a world where vampires and humans (mostly) coexist, later adapted on HBO as *True Blood.* In 2005, the first book in Stephenie Meyer's *Twilight* series turned vampires into a phenomenon once again (see sidebar, page 24).

Through it all, vampires have shown incredible staying power. More than 120 years after Bram Stoker published the novel that would immortalize *him* (the irony!), our obsession with the undead provides endless thrills for a thirsty public. ■

DRACULA'S DOG
1977

WESLEY SNIPES, IN *BLADE*
1998

HOW *TRUE BLOOD* AND *TWILIGHT* MADE VAMPIRES MODERN

In Charlaine Harris' 2001 book *Dead Until Dark*, a psychic named Sookie Stackhouse lives in a world shared by humans and vampires. That novel evolved into a 13-book series that sold millions of copies. In 2008, Harris' characters came to HBO in a series called *True Blood*. This revision of the genre took full advantage of premium cable, going heavy on the sex and nudity. It also explored the love triangle between Sookie (who turned out to be part fairy) and two vampires. Fans and critics liked the show: it won awards and lasted seven seasons.

In 2005, Stephenie Meyer's new vampire vision truly ignited the best-seller lists. Starting with that year's *Twilight* (and followed by *New Moon*, *Eclipse* and *Breaking Dawn*), her books were a huge draw for young adults, who reveled in the chaste sexiness.

They also liked the love triangle between a teenage girl, a vampire and a werewolf. Suddenly, every preteen and teenager—and many an older fan—was debating Bella's pros and cons, siding either with Team Edward (the vampire) or Team Jacob (the werewolf).

Starting in 2008, the movies made stars of Kristen Stewart (Bella) and Robert Pattinson (Edward), eventually becoming a five-film franchise that grossed more than $3.3 billion worldwide. A decade after the last book's release, *Twilight* still defines vampires for a new generation.

MICHAEL SHEEN, IN THE *TWILIGHT* SAGA
2008-12

KRISTEN STEWART AND ROBERT PATTINSON, IN THE *TWILIGHT* SAGA
2008-12

ANNA PAQUIN AND
STEPHEN MOYER, IN
TRUE BLOOD
2008–14

Anna Paquin and
Stephen Moyer
had such good
chemistry on
True Blood, they
fell in love and
married in 2010.

25

FRANKENSTEIN, 1931

FRANKENSTEIN

BRIDE OF FRANKENSTEIN, 1935

THE CREATURE FROM LAKE GENEVA

MARY SHELLEY WAS JUST 18 WHEN SHE DREAMED UP FRANKENSTEIN'S MONSTER, A NIGHTMARISH VISION THAT HAUNTS US TO THIS DAY.

It was a little over two centuries ago, on a rainy June night in 1816. In a rented house near Switzerland's Lake Geneva, 18-year-old Mary Godwin—soon to marry poet Percy Bysshe Shelley, who had already fathered her infant—was challenged to come up with a truly scary story. Shelley was there, as were the celebrated romantic poet George Lord Byron; Byron's personal physician, John Polidori; and Mary's stepsister, Claire, who had recently had an affair with Byron.

The group had been spending nights entertaining each other with discussions of science and philosophy, until the night Byron proposed, chiefly as a challenge to Shelley, that each of them invent a ghost story. The two poets soon tired of the effort, and it was Mary Godwin and John Polidori who rose to the challenge. His tale of a vampire would become the short novel *The Vampyre*. After several nights of coming up empty, Mary finally came up with a doozy.

"I saw the pale student of unhallowed arts kneeling beside the thing he had put together. I saw the hideous phantasm of a man stretched out and then, on the working of some powerful engine, show signs of life and stir with an uneasy, half-vital motion." That's from her 1831 preface to a revised edition of the book that would make her a legend. In that preface, she goes on to describe the rest of the dream, which held the keys to the full plot of the book. The book was *Frankenstein; Or, the Modern Prometheus*.

Mary's journal shows that she'd had another dream the previous February, shortly after losing her first infant. In it, her "little baby came back to life" after she'd

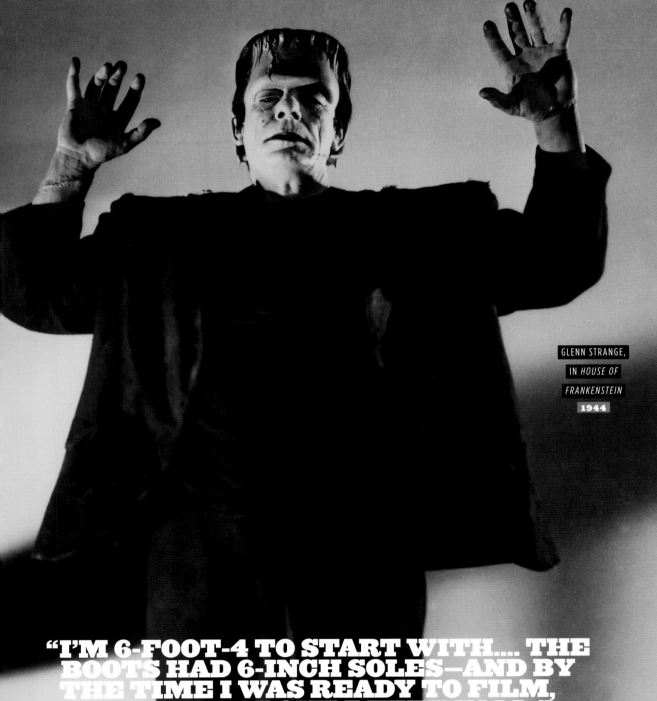

"I'M 6-FOOT-4 TO START WITH.... THE BOOTS HAD 6-INCH SOLES—AND BY THE TIME I WAS READY TO FILM, I WAS JUST ABOUT 7 FEET TALL."
—Glenn Strange

"THE MONSTER
WAS THE
BEST FRIEND
I EVER HAD."

—Boris Karloff

BORIS KARLOFF,
IN *FRANKENSTEIN*
1931

rubbed the tiny corpse by a fire till it heated up. Tragedy was to dog her throughout the writing of the book. One of her sisters committed suicide in October, and Percy's estranged, pregnant wife drowned herself that December. Mary, now 19, married Percy the same month. In May 1817 she finished writing *Frankenstein*, and it was published in March 1818, when she was 20.

A variety of sources inspired her, including the Roman poet Ovid's "Metamorphoses," in which the Greek god Prometheus angers Zeus by making a man in a god's image. Note, also, that her title refers not to the Creature but to its maker. She also drew on John Milton's *Paradise Lost* and on the *golem* of Jewish folklore, an animated clay anthropoid.

Literature and folklore were just the start. She was also inspired by German alchemist Johann Konrad Dippel (1673–1734), who performed experiments with dead animals and disinterred corpses. And there was the concept of Galvanism, which was then popular. In 1791, Bolognese physiologist Luigi Galvani wrote his *Commentary on the Effect of Electricity on Muscular Motion*. He concluded that animal tissue contains a "vital force." Soon known as Galvanism, the concept was similar to how Victor Frankenstein brings his Creature to life—by harnessing lightning's electric power.

Whatever her influences, Shelley's masterpiece is truly timeless. Because a work this old has long since entered the public domain, it is impossible to say how many people have read it. But if any character might rival

ABBOTT AND COSTELLO MEET FRANKENSTEIN 1948

PETER BOYLE, IN *YOUNG FRANKENSTEIN* 1974

MARY SHELLEY

Elsa Lanchester did double duty in *The Bride of Frankenstein*, playing both Mary Shelley and the Bride herself.

ELSA LANCHESTER, IN *THE BRIDE OF FRANKENSTEIN* 1935

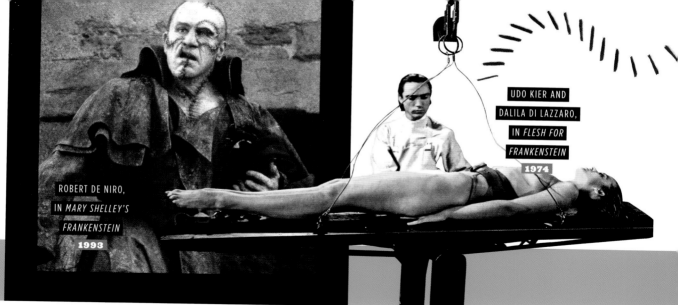

Dracula as the most famous in horror, it would be Victor Frankenstein's Creature. The very name Frankenstein inspires images of death and rebirth, of a mad scientist, of violations against nature itself. We pity and fear the scared, confused monster as he roams the countryside looking for someplace to call home and even as he flees an angry mob wielding pitchforks and blazing torches.

A loss of love, a rejection of fatherhood, the tragedy and terror of being utterly and completely alone in the world—they all combine to make this one of the saddest and most chilling of all monster tales. Many stories rely on scares and the supernatural, but only Frankenstein's story combines those so powerfully with the monster's own pathos. In that 1831 preface, Shelley wrote that she

had wished to tell a tale that would "speak to the mysterious fears of our nature and awaken thrilling horror." Boy, did she. Two centuries later, the tale of Frankenstein is one of the most famous in all of literature, adapted again and again in books, in film, in theater and on television.

In 1910, Charles Edison's film studio made the earliest movie of Shelley's tale, a 16-minute silent titled *Frankenstein*. Two other filmed adaptations have been lost. Director James Whale's *Frankenstein* became the first major adaptation, released on November 21, 1931. Starring Boris Karloff (plus 48 pounds of makeup, costume and boots) as the Creature, it came out nine months after Tod Browning's *Dracula*. Though it adapted only part of the novel, the film was a smash. The 1930s horror era was underway.

Whale made a sequel four years later, *The Bride of Frankenstein*, which is considered one of the greatest horror films ever. Based on later sections of the novel, it featured Elsa Lanchester (and her trademark two-tone hair) as the dead woman who is brought back to life to keep the Creature company—but rejects him.

Many movies followed. Soon, Frankenstein's monster was co-starring with Dracula, the Wolf Man and, of course, the legendary comedy team of Abbott and Costello (in 1948's *Abbott and Costello Meet Frankenstein*). Dozens more followed over the years, including seven from Britain's Hammer Films plus Mel Brooks' hilarious comedic take on the story (*Young Frankenstein*); exploitations like *Frankenstein Meets the Space Monster* and

Jesse James Meets Frankenstein's Daughter; literary approaches from Oscar-winning creators like Guillermo del Toro and Kenneth Branagh; artsy concepts, like Andy Warhol's *Flesh for Frankenstein*; and even Tim Burton's animated tale of a young boy and his reanimated dog: *Frankenweenie.* This list barely scratches the surface.

Shelley's creation transcends literature and even popular culture. It conjures vividly real dreamscapes and nightmares that have pursued people for thousands of years. And it appears that two centuries after she wrote her masterwork, Mary Shelley remains far ahead of her time. ■

FRANKENSTEIN MEETS SPACE MONSTER
1965

FRANKENWEENIE
2012

DANNY BOYLE STAGES A MASTERPIECE

In 2011, Oscar-winning director Danny Boyle brought a production of *Frankenstein* to the London stage. It was not the first time Mary Shelley's book had been adapted for that medium: *Presumption; or, the Fate of Frankenstein*, by Richard Brinsley Peake, premiered at the English Opera House in London in 1823, just five years after the novel was published.

In the nearly two centuries since, there had been Broadway adaptations and musicals as well as smaller productions, but it was Boyle's version, adapted by Nick Dear from Shelley's novel, that really caught the public's attention.

Respected actors Benedict Cumberbatch and Jonny Lee Miller played both Frankenstein and the Creature, swapping the roles nightly. Unlike most movies, which focus on the creation of the monster and the panic he sparks, this play went far deeper into the novel. It followed Frankenstein's Creature as he learns to speak, read and write, which leads to his tragic understanding of his own creation.

Rejected wherever he goes, the Creature eventually disappears. Victor Frankenstein tracks his creation down in the Alps and agrees to create a female partner for him. But once he does, he has second thoughts and destroys her, leading the Creature to swear revenge. This leads to more horror and madness and a very tragic ending.

For their performances, Cumberbatch and Miller shared every major British theater award—including the Olivier, the British version of the Tony. The show was so popular, a performance was broadcast around the world in March 2011, in the midst of the play's three-month run. (Sadly, it is not currently available.)

Actors Benedict
Cumberbatch (main,
left) and Jonny Lee
Miller swapped stage
roles nightly.

03

AN AMERICAN WEREWOLF IN LONDON, 1981

WEREWOLVES

WILD
AT HEART

**HALF MAN, HALF BEAST, ALL MONSTER.
DECODING THE PEDIGREE AND POWER OF OUR
MOST ANCIENT AND PRIMORDIAL FIEND.**

Unlike the Count, with his elegant horror, and Frankenstein's Creature, whom we pity and fear, werewolves seem so primitive—all fur and teeth and noise. Why do we keep coming back to them? What makes them so terrifying? Perhaps it's because they're so primal and real, like something dark that we keep squashed down deep within ourselves.

Werewolves (men who become wolves) and wolf men (who take on wolfish qualities but walk upright) go back tens of thousands of years, to cave paintings in southern France. Of all monsters, they are most primordially plugged into human fears, because the werewolf idea

resonates with the beast within us all. And the idea that such a creature might attack you in the dark? That fear speaks to real, ancient dangers.

"We looked at art that goes back to the dawn of humanity and found it had one common feature: animal-human hybrids," according to Cambridge University's Dr. Christopher Chippindale. "Werewolves and vampires are as old as art, in other words. These composite beings, from a world between humans and animals, are a common theme from the beginning of painting."

Through the centuries, these hairy hybrids show up in folklore

David Naughton
is unrecognizable
in the 1981 classic
*An American
Werewolf in London.*

again and again. A partial list starts 4,000 years ago, with the *Epic of Gilgamesh*, which featured a hairy character named Enkidu. In Greek mythology, King Lycaon's bad temper got him turned into a wolf—and gave us the word *lycan*. The Greek historian Herodotus described a race of people who become wolves once a year. If his geography is correct, the Neuri lived in what would become the Slavic homeland, which would give Slavic werewolf stories truly deep roots. The Roman poet Virgil wrote about Moeris, a man who turned into a wolf after using herbs. Uh-huh. Herbs.

It goes on: In the fifth century, St. Patrick is said to have turned a Welsh king into a wolf and then cursed whole tribes of unbelievers to become wolves. In the 13th-century Icelandic *Saga of the Volsunds*, magic wolf skins turn their wearers into wolves for 10 days. The Cóir Anmann, an ancient Irish text, features stories about warrior-werewolves.

And then there's France. In the 16th century, various Frenchmen killed and ate children and adults, claiming they could turn into wolves. In ensuing centuries, thousands of French people were charged with the same condition. The story of Little Red Riding Hood, which features a villainous

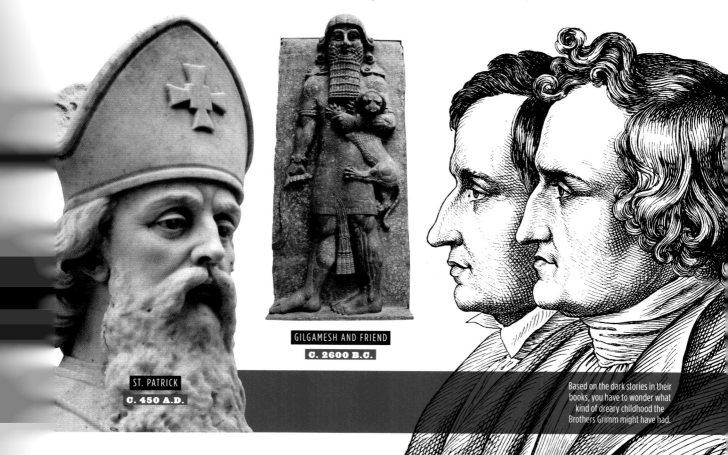

GILGAMESH AND FRIEND
C. 2600 B.C.

ST. PATRICK
C. 450 A.D.

Based on the dark stories in their books, you have to wonder what kind of dreary childhood the Brothers Grimm might have had.

"THE WOLF MAN DIDN'T WANT TO DO ALL THOSE BAD THINGS. HE WAS FORCED INTO THEM."

—Lon Chaney Jr.

Lon Chaney Jr. played Lawrence Talbot, aka the Wolf Man, four times. Here, he puts the fear in Elena Verdugo in *House of Frankenstein* (1944).

HOW TO KILL IT

A SILVER BULLET TO THE HEART ▶

werewolf, was published in 1697 in France and adapted by the Brothers Grimm in 1812. In the 1840s, G. W. M. Reynolds wrote his serialized *Wagner, the Wehr-Wolf*, about a man who trades his soul to the devil for immortality and power. The cost? He becomes a werewolf every seven years.

Kooky as it sounds, science may help explain this. Hypertrichosis produces excessive hair growth over the entire body. The disease porphyria can bring on trances, seizures and hallucinations. Schizophrenia can bring on feelings of animalistic savagery. Also—and this may be the kicker—ergot, a fungus found in moldy rye, may have caused mass hallucinations. LSD was first made from ergot in a lab in 1943. And then, there are always...herbs.

Yet lycanthropy didn't grip the American psyche until 1941, when Universal Pictures released *The Wolf Man*, starring Lon Chaney Jr. There had been two previous attempts, a silent film in 1913 and *Werewolf of London* in 1935, but it was this film, 10 years into the horror boom, that

The **WOLF MAN**

with
Claude RAINS   Warren WILLIAM
Ralph BELLAMY   Patric KNOWLES
Bela LUGOSI   Maria OUSPENSKAYA
Evelyn ANKERS
and Lon CHANEY

Lon Chaney Jr. made his name in monster movies, following in the footsteps of his father, Lon Chaney Sr., who was one of the biggest stars of the silent movie era.

I Was A Teenage Werewolf was released as a double feature in 1957 with *Invasion of the Saucer Men.*

made a real impact. The main character returns from the States to his ancestral castle in England. He takes an interest in a local shopgirl and buys an unusual walking stick from her. They go strolling through a gypsy camp at night with her friend and meet a fortune-teller and her son. The son seems normal, but soon turns into a werewolf and kills the friend. The hero kills the werewolf with his silver-handled stick, but gets bitten—and that's where his troubles begin.

Like Boris Karloff did for *Frankenstein*, Chaney had to sit still for four hours at a time while makeup was applied. The filmed transformations, shot in reverse order a few frames at a time, took all day. Tiny nails held his hands in place against starched fabric to ensure realism. Even so, Chaney looks underdone compared to modern werewolves, since only his head, hands and feet ever change.

After this, the Wolf Man never appeared again in a film as the sole monster; in all subsequent outings he battled Universal Pictures' other creatures. That's probably because he came to life toward the end of the horror craze, just when Universal started

MICHAEL J. FOX, IN *TEEN WOLF* 1985

ELISABETH BROOKS, IN *THE HOWLING* 1981

combining its menagerie—with titles like *Frankenstein Meets the Wolf Man*—to boost interest.

In the years since, various versions of the tale, including the teen horror flick *I Was a Teenage Werewolf,* in 1957, and Hammer's *The Curse of the Werewolf,* in 1961, have made it to the big screen.

The '80s were a good decade for horror—and for werewolves especially. In 1981 alone, *The Howling, Wolfen* and *An American Werewolf in London* hit screens. Based on a novel by Gary Brandner, *The Howling* was directed by future *Gremlins* helmer Joe Dante; it went on to spawn seven sequels. The stylish thriller *Wolfen* was based on the 1978 novel by Whitley Strieber, whose vampire book, *The Hunger,* also became a movie (see page 23). John Landis, who directed *Animal House* in 1978, had been working on his story for more than a decade before success enabled him to make *An American Werewolf in London.* Dante's and Landis' hits led to major breakthroughs in special effects (see sidebar, page 47). They also developed huge cult followings.

The Michael J. Fox comedy *Teen Wolf* hit theaters in 1985, six weeks after another Fox movie, a little

A HOWLING GOOD HIT SONG

Any discussion of werewolves must pay respect to the late Warren Zevon's biggest hit, "Werewolves of London." The 1978 song, which he called "a dumb song for smart people," sports lyrics like "I saw Lon Chaney Jr. walking with the queen/Doing the werewolves of London." Dumb or not, it made him a star. A classic-rock staple, it's been covered and sampled and used in many movies, and it remains popular on the radio. *AH-HOOOOO!*

Rick Baker received a star on the Hollywood Walk of Fame in 2012.

RICK BAKER, SPECIAL-EFFECTS WIZARD

It's one thing to be good at your job. It's another thing to be *so* good that you help inspire the Academy of Motion Picture Arts and Sciences to create a whole new award. Such is the legend of Rick Baker, an expert in makeup and special effects who won a record seven Oscars—including the very first statuette for makeup, awarded in 1981 for his work on *An American Werewolf in London*.

Baker first fell in love with making unique looks as a teenager, when he began creating artificial body parts in his parents' kitchen. He broke into the business, at age 22, as an assistant on *The Exorcist* before moving on to projects like the 1976 remake of *King Kong*, in which he not only designed the giant ape but played him, too.

But Baker really made his bones while working for director John Landis. In 1981, the makeup Baker designed for actor David Naughton—the titular werewolf—was astonishing. It became both the film's lasting legacy and his own. He even helped come up with the special effect of the transformation, changing Naughton from a human to a werewolf long before CGI. They pulled hair through fake body parts and then reversed the film to make the hair appear to grow rather than recede. Sounds simple now, but at the time, it was groundbreaking.

Baker's career spanned more than four decades, and he retired after the 2014 Disney film *Maleficent*. His final Oscar win? That was in 2011, for *The Wolfman*.

RICK BAKER, IN FULL MADE-UP GLORY, IN 2010

MICHELLE PFEIFFER, IN *LADYHAWKE*
1985

KATE BECKINSALE, IN *UNDERWORLD*
2003

SCOTT SPEEDMAN, IN *UNDERWORLD*
2003

GINGER SNAPS
2002

thing called *Back to the Future*. Though his star was on the rise, Fox's blockbuster overshadowed his furry little teen comedy at the box office. It soon won a major cult following on home video, however, and was reincarnated as a long-running TV show in 2011.

Later in 1985, an adaptation of the Stephen King novel *Silver Bullet* was released, with a screenplay by King himself. Also that year, the Michelle Pfeiffer fantasy *Ladyhawke* featured a man who transforms into a wolf at night. Werewolves ran amok in sequels and low-budget movies for the rest of the decade—but it wasn't until 1994 that a major

actor actually played a lycan, when Jack Nicholson starred in the drama *Wolf*.

Released in 2001, *Ginger Snaps* is a truly scary movie about twin sisters and uses lycanthropy as a bloody metaphor for adolescence. The 2004 sequel went even darker and is beloved by fans. In 2002's *Dog Soldiers*, British soldiers in training find themselves battling werewolves on the highlands in Scotland.

Oddly, it wasn't till 2003 that someone made a big-budget modern movie pitting vampires against lycans, but director Len Wiseman and star Kate Beckinsale did just that in the

thriller *Underworld*; the fifth installment came out in 2016.

Werewolves and vampires also shared the screen in the *Twilight* movies and on HBO's *True Blood* (see page 24). The latest lycan outing, *The Wolfman*, starring Benicio del Toro and Anthony Hopkins, flopped in 2010, though many loved it.

Somehow, the monster with the deepest history and realest origins is among the least popular, but longevity conveys power. The werewolf and Wolf Man are pop-culture staples, though they may never be as dominant as bloodsuckers and other invented creatures. ▬

Benicio del Toro starred in 2010's *The Wolfman*; it was makeup wiz Rick Baker's last movie.

"THAT WAS NOT EASY.... IF I WANTED TO SAY SOMETHING, THEY HAD TO TAKE OUT MY TEETH."

—Benicio del Toro

04

THE MUMMY, 1959

CREATURE FROM THE BLACK LAGOON, 1954

MUMMIES & OTHER CREEPS

MONSTER
MASH

FROM ANCIENT EGYPT TO THE BLACK LAGOON AND FROM GREMLINS TO ONE VERY SCARY CLOWN AND THE BLOB, TERROR COMES IN A VARIETY OF FORMS.

Bloodsuckers, composite people, vulpine marauders and the supernatural have generally taken horror's center stage, joined in the past few decades by zombies, slashers and other modern terrors. But scares come in many shapes and sizes. This chapter is about other awful outsiders that stalk the imagination.

Mummies, for example, are a peculiar type of monster. They are undead, they are ancient, and they are usually Egyptian. (Some come from south of the border, but they're less popular.) Mummies are not mindless, like zombies, or bloodthirsty shape-shifters, like vampires. They don't run; they shuffle. Are they creepy? Absolutely.

The act of mummification itself is not terribly spooky or supernatural. It's simply the preservation of a person (or animal) by exposure to chemicals, cold, low humidity or a general lack of air. So what makes a mummy a monster? Generally, it's an ancient curse that lands on anyone dopey enough to disturb a mummy. The mummy becomes reanimated, and all bets are off. Very Bad Things happen.

The word mummy comes from the Latin *mumia*, which comes from the Arabic *mumiya* and the Persian *mum*, meaning wax. The Egyptians were mummifying, or embalming, their dead since before 3500 B.C., though the earliest known mentions of undead mummies lie in an 1827 novel by Jane C. Loudon called *The Mummy!: Or a Tale of the Twenty-Second Century*. It's pretty much what the title suggests: A mummy comes back to life in the future. Other mummy lit includes *Lost in a Pyramid; or, The Mummy's*

Rachel Weisz, Brendan Fraser and a whole lot of CGI reawakened *The Mummy* for the big screen in 1999.

"I GUESS DARKNESS SERVES A PURPOSE: TO SHOW US THAT THERE IS REDEMPTION THROUGH CHAOS."

—Brendan Fraser

Curse, an 1869 short story by *Little Women* author Louisa May Alcott, as well as Bram Stoker's 1903 novel *The Jewel of the Seven Stars.*

The big event that made mummies mainstream was archaeologist Howard Carter's discovery of King Tut's tomb in 1922. Within a decade, the Mummy was on the big screen, part of the cinematic horror boom that Universal Pictures had begun in 1931, with *Dracula* and then *Frankenstein.* Boris Karloff, who had just played Frankenstein's monster, starred in *The Mummy* as Imhotep, an ancient Egyptian brought back to life and searching for his lost love. Another four Mummy movies followed over the next dozen years, sputtering to a laughable end with *Abbott and Costello Meet the Mummy* in 1955.

Hammer Films (see sidebar, right) released more Mummy movies in the 1950s and '60s, but even in these works, the character never had the same weight as its monster brethren. (Even the Wolf Man has had more appearances in pop culture.)

But that doesn't mean the Mummy isn't scary. The concept of an ancient curse coming for you, in the form of an evil-looking figure bandaged from head to foot, is more than a little unnerving. If you doubt it, observe the enormous success of the 1999 horror adventure *The Mummy.* That movie spawned a four-film

HAMMER'S HOLD ON HORROR

Founded in 1934, England's Hammer Films did sci-fi, film noir, comedies, thrillers and even an adaptation of the Sherlock Holmes story *The Hound of the Baskervilles,* starring Peter Cushing. It rode the midcentury sci-fi craze till its end, then had a smash with *The Curse of Frankenstein* in 1956.

In 1958, Universal Studios agreed to let Hammer remake all the horror movies in Universal's library. Hammer made six Frankenstein movies; 14 vampire movies (eight starring Dracula); three Mummy movies; and other scary titles like *The Abominable Snowman, The Two Faces of Dr. Jekyll* (and *Dr. Jekyll and Sister Hyde*), *The Curse of the Werewolf, The Phantom of the Opera* (before it was a Broadway musical), *The Gorgon, The Plague of the Zombies* and *The Reptile.*

The company essentially went out of business in the 1980s, but in 2007 it resumed production under new ownership. Hammer has released seven movies in the past decade, highlighted by 2010's *Let Me In* (based on the Swedish tween vampire love story *Let the Right One In*) and 2012's *The Woman in Black,* a well-received gothic ghost story starring Daniel Radcliffe and Ciaran Hinds.

Just a year after becoming a star in 1931's *Frankenstein*, Boris Karloff branched out to play the Mummy.

55

series that made more than $1.4 billion worldwide and launched the film career of Dwayne "The Rock" Johnson. He played not a Mummy but the Scorpion King (all man above the waist, all CGI scorpion below). Though the 2017 reboot starring Tom Cruise disappointed and won't see a sequel, there's no denying the power of the ancient Mummy.

Now let's leave Egypt and head stateside, where a different kind of curse invaded movie screens—and millions of nightmares—in 1984. Joe Dante's horror-comedy *Gremlins* had a brilliant concept: This cuddly little creature will be fine, as long as you follow three simple rules. First, no bright light. Second, don't get it wet. Third and most important, do not, under any circumstances, ever, *ever*, feed it after midnight. Of course, as soon as those rules are broken—as they inevitably will be—say goodbye to friends, family and most of

your town, since an army of evil creatures will tear them all apart. The sequel was less successful, but the Gremlins legend lives on, more than three decades later.

We could do an entire book about creepy clowns, but there's one smiling killer who owns the genre. He exists in an alternate reality and shows up in the same cursed Maine town every 28 years to terrorize children. Stephen King introduced Pennywise in a 1986 novel. While *It* the book was a best seller, *It* the 1990 TV miniseries was a sensation. And then, in 2017, *It* the movie made more than $700 million worldwide. And the 2019 sequel, *It Chapter Two*, drew up even more scares and delights.

While humanoid fish creatures and oversize amoebas may *seem* less intimidating, *Creature From the Black Lagoon* and *The Blob* were both huge horror hits in the 1950s. The former was a fish-

human hybrid that arose from dark waters to terrorize a group of explorers. The Blob was an alien that crash-landed in suburban Pennsylvania and ate everything in its path. Both became punch lines over the years, but the Creature recently got some serious love (see sidebar, page 54), and *The Blob* gave us one of screen legend Steve McQueen's first starring roles. They're sort of in the same category as a mummy: something we think of as scary—but only under certain circumstances, and, well, at the end of the day, not really. ◼

GREMLINS
1984

SOFIA BOUTELLA, IN *THE MUMMY*
2017

BILL SKARSGÅRD, IN *IT*
2017

THE MUMMY
1999

A mummy discovered by three Egyptologists comes back to life and takes his revenge in Hammer Films' 1964 *The Curse of the Mummy's Tomb*.

HOW *THE SHAPE OF WATER* WON THE CREATURE SOME RESPECT

Few horror fans think much of the 1954 B movie *The Creature from the Black Lagoon*. Generally speaking, devotees aside, it's seen as an exploitation flick starring a stuntman in a comical rubber fish suit who scares a boatload of folks on the Amazon River. The movie is not even 80 minutes long, and its plot is as twist-free as a ruler. For more than six decades, there was no reason to treat the creature or its movie as much more than a joke—again, devotees aside.

But Guillermo del Toro, known for such thoughtful horror as *Pan's Labyrinth*, *Crimson Peak* and TV's *The Strain*, was one such devotee, and in 2017, his *The Shape of Water* changed the creature forever. Set in the early 1960s, at the height of the Cold War, the film is a gorgeously shot, beautifully told love story between a mute cleaning woman and a creature pulled from the Amazon by U.S. agents. From humble origins came a rich and layered tale of humanity and how it often thrives in places we don't expect. Nominated for 13 Oscars in 2018, the movie won four, including Best Picture and Best Director for del Toro. After more than half a century, the poor, rubbery creature finally got his due.

RICOU BROWNING AND
SALLY HAWKINS, IN
THE SHAPE OF WATER
2017

Two actors played the Creature: Ben Chapman on land and Ricou Browning in water.

05

THE WALKING DEAD, 2010

ZOMBIES

UNDEAD
AND BIGGER THAN EVER
ARE WE AT PEAK ZOMBIE? FROM VOODOO TO ZOM-ROM-COMS, WE JUST CANNOT GET ENOUGH OF THE LIVING, WALKING DEAD.

Who doesn't love a good zombie story? These days, zombies are among the most popular forms of horror. Why are the undead so hot? Maybe it's because we like to imagine how we'd respond if we had to face them. Maybe it's because so many people these days just act like zombies, even if they're still (technically) alive.

Before we get into modern zombie horror, let's explore the roots of this phenomenon. The word *zombi* comes from voodoo, a mostly Haitian religion that involves witchcraft, magic, raising the dead and animal sacrifices. Perhaps that's why voodoo practitioners don't see the zombie the way many pop culture fans do: as the building blocks of a cataclysmic event that could bring an end to society as we know it.

The *Oxford English Dictionary* says the word *zombie* comes from West Africa, comparing it to Kongo words *nzambi* (god) and *zombi* (fetish). In 1929, W. B. Seabrook wrote *The Magic Island*, a book about his travels in Haiti. It was among the first to introduce Westerners to the concept: "The *zombie*, they say, is a soulless human corpse, still dead but taken from the grave and endowed by sorcery with a mechanical semblance of life."

Apart from voodoo, the literary history of zombies, or reanimated dead folks, goes back to Mary Shelley's *Frankenstein*. It also shows up in H. P. Lovecraft's work and even plays a part in Richard Matheson's 1954 novella, *I Am Legend*, where humanity has been wiped out by a zombie-meets-vampires virus. (Will Smith starred in the 2007 movie adaptation.) All of these books drew on European folklore about the undead.

The Serpent and the Rainbow author Wade Davis sold the rights only on the condition that Peter Weir would direct and Mel Gibson would star. In the end, Wes Craven directed and Bill Pullman (above, choked by a monster) starred.

63

The genre's first movie was *White Zombie*, directed by Victor Halperin in 1932. Bela Lugosi played an evil voodoo master in Haiti who not only controls zombie slaves but murders and then revives a young American woman as...a zombie! This film set the tone and de facto "rules" for about two dozen zombie movies over the next 35 years, including *I Walked With a Zombie* and even Ed Wood's legendary 1959 masterpiece of awfulness, *Plan 9 from Outer Space*. The scares in *Invasion of the Body Snatchers* (1956) came from watching friends and family become zombie-like automatons, hosts to alien occupiers. Zombies in other films of this era came from all over: outer space, undersea, graves around the world and, of course, the Caribbean.

Everything changed in 1968, when George Romero released his classic *Night of the Living Dead* (see page 72). At least partly inspired by Matheson's work, it was the first movie to show us zombies as we have long imagined them: slow and mindless yet unstoppable in their quest for human flesh. The word "zombie" is never spoken, but fans later used it to describe the undead.

It took Romero 10 years to release a sequel, *Dawn of the Dead*, which he made with Italian horror master Dario Argento. In that time, more than two dozen zombie movies were made, some

28 Days Later gave us something new: fast zombies! Run for your lives!

MILLA JOVOVICH, IN *RESIDENT EVIL* 2002

SHARON CECCATTI, IN
DAWN OF THE DEAD
1978

Dawn of the Dead took dead aim at consumerism. The survivors escape to a mall, where they feel safe—underscoring the importance Americans placed on products.

65

PET SEMATARY
1989

The 1989 film *Pet Sematary* was a huge hit, but the 2019 remake got only a so-so response.

even using the words "living dead" in the title. Romero would go on to make four more sequels, but the original was his finest hour.

The 1980s were a good time for horror, and zombies feasted at this trough of gore and terror. You don't get much more mainstream than the zombie dance scene in Michael Jackson's 1983 "Thriller" video, but zombies starred in dozens of '80s movies. Some of the biggest or most pedigreed were *C.H.U.D.* (1984); Stuart Gordon's *Re-Animator* and Tobe Hooper's *Lifeforce* (both 1985); Wes Craven's *The Serpent and the Rainbow* (1988); and *Pet Sematary* (1989), based on the 1983 Stephen King novel of the same name. In 1992, Peter Jackson, famous today for his *Lord of the Rings* trilogy, made a zombie comedy called *Dead Alive*.

In 2002, zombies roared back in two hit films. *Resident Evil*, starring Milla Jovovich as a hot body fighting rotting bodies, spawned five sequels (the last was in 2017). In *28 Days Later*, British director Danny Boyle introduced both a fresh perspective and "fast zombies." Suddenly, the living dead weren't just shuffling along—they were running and jumping and chasing live prey in a fashion far scarier than what we'd seen before.

"I was on the fence about zombies, to be honest," Boyle told Yahoo! Movies when the film was

MICHAEL JACKSON, IN THE VIDEO FOR "THRILLER" 1983

WILL SMITH, IN *I AM LEGEND* 2007

LIFE F
198

A recent article in a New York newspaper reported that there were large colonies of people living under the city...

The paper was incorrect. What is living under the city is not human.

C.H.U.D. is under the city.

They're not staying down *there*, anymore!

C.H.U.D.
(Cannibalistic. Humanoid. Underground. Dwellers.)

ANDREW BONIME presents JOHN HEARD DANIEL STERN CHRISTOPHER CURRY C.H.U.D.
Director of Photography PETER STEIN Screenplay by PARNELL HALL Story by SHEPARD ABBOTT
Produced by ANDREW BONIME Directed by DOUGLAS CHEEK

released. "I found them a bit daft. And I used to joke, 'You can just walk away from them. Why does everyone panic? A quick-tempo walk, and you're free! It's not a problem.'" He certainly solved that non-problem. In 2007, Boyle's film spawned a sequel, *28 Weeks Later*. Legal snafus are holding up a second sequel, which would likely have the word "months" in its title.

More fast zombies appeared in a 2004 remake of Romero's *Dawn of the Dead*, the directorial debut of Zack Snyder, who would later helm such films as *300*, *Man of Steel* and *Justice League*. The year 2004 also saw what might be the first zombie romantic comedy, or zom-rom-com. *Shaun of the Dead* (see sidebar, right) is still considered one of the best examples of the genre it mocks.

Thanks to those films in the first years of this century, the zeitgeist was primed for zombies to go mainstream. In 2011, even the United States Centers for Disease Control and Prevention—yes, the actual government agency—published a graphic novel on its website called *Preparedness 101: Zombie Apocalypse.*

So when Robert Kirkman's hit comic book *The Walking Dead* became an AMC TV series in 2010, it soon became one of the most-watched shows on TV. Not just on cable, mind you, but on *all* television, reaching almost 16 million viewers in season five.

ZOM-COMS: HOW SHAUN LAUGHED AT THE END OF THE WORLD

Just because the world is coming to an end doesn't mean we can't all have a laugh. That's why a movie like *Shaun of the Dead*—co-written by, and starring, Britain's Simon Pegg—can be considered one of the best zombie movies ever made, even though it skewers the genre in a most meta fashion. Like the best satire, it embraces and exemplifies the very thing it mocks.

The 2009 zom-com *Zombieland* similarly aimed a jaundiced eye at a postapocalyptic America, where a handful of survivors try to find some companionship. Like the original *Dawn of the Dead*, it too spears commercialism and pop culture. It's funnier than it sounds (especially Bill Murray's long cameo), but it features a controversial take on zombies first seen in *28 Days Later* and then in the *Dawn of the Dead* remake: fast zombies. Pegg, for one, is not a fan of such things.

In a 2008 op-ed for the *Guardian*, a U.K. newspaper, he wrote, "I know it is absurd to debate the rules of a reality that does not exist, but this genuinely irks me. You cannot kill a vampire with an MDF [fiberboard] stake; werewolves can't fly; zombies do not run. It's a misconception, a bastardization that diminishes a classic movie monster."

If anyone should know, it's him, right?

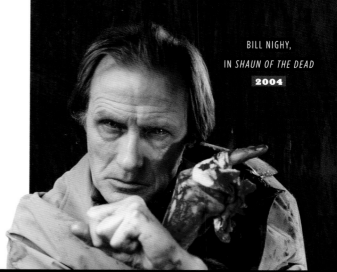

BILL NIGHY, IN *SHAUN OF THE DEAD* **2004**

SIMON PEGG,
IN *SHAUN OF THE DEAD*
2004

In 2020, *Shaun of the Dead* co-writer and star Simon Pegg recorded a popular PSA for the COVID-19 crisis with co-star Nick Frost.

LUCY DAVIS, KATE ASHFIELD, DYLAN MORAN, SIMON PEGG,
PENELOPE WILTON AND NICK FROST, IN *SHAUN OF THE DEAD*
2004

THE WALKING DEAD
2010

The comic-book industry was rocked in 2019 when *The Walking Dead* comic creator Robert Kirkman said he had no more ideas for stories to tell.

Brad Pitt starred in and co-produced *World War Z*. Here, he's prepping for the worst with Mireille Enos and little Sterling Jerins.

HOW TO KILL IT

YOU HAVE TO CRUSH ITS SKULL

In 2015, it produced a spinoff, *Fear the Walking Dead*, and is still going strong.

There's also Max Brooks' best-selling 2006 novel, *World War Z*— an "oral history of the zombie war" in which a UN researcher travels the world talking to survivors of a zombie apocalypse that has almost wiped out humanity. It spawned a movie starring Brad Pitt, which came out in 2013—the same year another book adaptation, the zom-rom-com *Warm Bodies*, reached the big screen. Two years later, we got *iZombie*, a lighthearted TV series that was loosely adapted for The CW from a comic book.

Zombies...they're everywhere! In movies, on television, in books, and even in government media, we can't get enough of the undead—and the more they scare us, the better. ■

"ZOMBIE IN PURPLE SHIRT," IN *THE WALKING DEAD*
2010

FATHER OF THE MODERN ZOMBIE

Before George Romero made them mainstream, zombies weren't known for eating human flesh. His *Night of the Living Dead* fixed that, and then the 1985 horror comedy *Return of the Living Dead* (not his movie) specified that zombies really want to munch on brains. Romero also introduced the concept of the zombie apocalypse, a global outbreak that lays society low. This would soon become a staple of modern storytelling.

"The Romero movies as a whole, I really adore," says *The Walking Dead* creator Robert Kirkman. "*Day of the Dead* has more action and gore in it, while I think *Night of the Living Dead* is probably the most sophisticated zombie movie. It's got excellent story, an amazing ending and it's really artfully put together. It's obviously been a huge influence."

Romero's 1978 sequel, *Dawn of the Dead*, follows a group of survivors who have barricaded themselves in a mall to survive the crisis introduced in Romero's 1968 film. Not only was *Dawn* wildly popular as a straight horror film, it was hailed as a masterpiece of social satire, skewering modern consumerism, government ineptitude, bioengineering, greed and exploitation.

"A zombie film is not fun without a bunch of stupid people running around and [us]observing how they fail to handle the situation," Romero once said. "The neighbors are scary enough when they're not dead."

Romero made other films in his impressive career, but he was best known for his *Living Dead* movies, right up until his death in 2017 at the age of 77.

George Romero's innovation was to give zombies a very specific purpose: to eat brains. Also, to have them walk...very...slowly.

GEORGE ROMERO

THE EXORCIST, 1973

GHOSTS
AND OTHER CREEPY STORIES
HAUNTINGS, PHANTASMS, POSSESSION AND MORE UNEXPLAINABLE THINGS THAT GO BUMP IN THE NIGHT.

At some level, most horror deals with the supernatural, because, really, how else do you explain vampires, werewolves, monsters arisen from the dead and other terrors? Even the slasher genre, with its unkillable killers inhabiting dreams and menacing teenagers, is pretty supernatural. But here, we're talking about the paranormal—about ghostly spirits, devious demons, wicked witches and warlocks and everything in between.

The paranormal movie genre started in the 1920s, with German Expressionist films (e.g., *The Hands of Orlac)*, carried through the Universal movies of the 1930s and then, aside from some ghost movies of the 1950s (e.g., *House on Haunted Hill*), essentially ran out of steam. People didn't find that stuff scary anymore. The science fiction tales of the 1950s and early 1960s—which we'll cover in the next chapter—were more than enough to scare audiences. The supernatural had lost its mojo.

A couple of early 1960s exploitation films—*The Innocents* in 1961 and *The Haunting* in 1963—did break through. The former stars Deborah Kerr as an English governess who's convinced that the house where she works is haunted. In the latter, a scientist researching the paranormal invites two women—stars Julie Harris and Claire Bloom—to a haunted mansion, where one of the women starts to lose her mind. Both films have attained cult status and were highly influential.

In 1968, Roman Polanski made his American directorial debut

"TO BE HONEST, I WAS NOT ENTHUSIASTIC ABOUT HER UNTIL WE STARTED TO WORK. THEN I DISCOVERED, SOMEWHAT TO MY SURPRISE, THAT SHE IS A BRILLIANT ACTRESS."

—Roman Polanski on Mia Farrow in *Rosemary's Baby*

with *Rosemary's Baby*, based on the best-selling novel by Ira Levin. In it, an unsuspecting young housewife's husband makes a deal with the devil: He lets Satan impregnate his wife (Mia Farrow) in exchange for a successful career. Combining social commentary with abject terror, the film was a major hit and a later influence.

Things started to change in 1973. In August, in director Robin Hardy's *The Wicker Man*, a London police officer goes to the Scottish countryside to investigate a murder but gets tangled up with a witches' coven. While not an enormous hit, it set the table for the major change to come in December. That's when William Friedkin's adaptation of William Peter Blatty's novel *The Exorcist* exploded onto the scene, scaring the living daylights out of audiences and becoming a box-office sensation. Nearly five decades later, it remains the third-highest-grossing supernatural horror movie ever. The story of a girl possessed by a demon sent people into paroxysms of fear, with moviegoers fainting, crying and staggering out of screenings, shaken by the movie and, in particular, by the sight of Linda Blair's head spinning around a full 360 degrees.

Many film and horror fans believe *The Exorcist* remains the

Below: Pamela Franklin's Flora prays the Lord her soul to keep as Deborah Kerr's Miss Giddens looks on, in *The Innocents*.

That innocent-looking child is, in fact... the Antichrist! in the supernatural thriller *The Omen*.

HARVEY STEPHENS, GREGORY PECK AND LEE REMICK, IN *THE OMEN* 1976

Richard Johnson's Dr. Markway saves Julie Harris' Eleanor Lance from falling off a balcony in *The Haunting*.

"IT'S SORT OF A LAND *JAWS* FOR ME.... THE GREAT SIMILARITY IS THAT TERROR IS RELENTLESS, AND THE TERROR IS UNSEEN IN BOTH MOVIES [UNTIL THE END]."

—Steven Spielberg

HEATHER O'ROURKE, IN *POLTERGEIST*
1982

scariest movie ever made. But more than that, it was a cultural sensation. Not since the Universal films of the early 1930s had horror so pervaded the mainstream. A financial and critical success, Friedkin's film earned 10 Academy Award nominations and took home two Oscars (for Adapted Screenplay and Sound Design).

Shortly after, in January 1974, director Nicolas Roeg's *Don't Look Now*, starring Donald Sutherland and Julie Christie as a couple dealing with the loss of their daughter, carried forward this mysterious and spiritual genre. The movie turns very dark very quickly and is known for the extremely realistic sex scene between the two stars. It piqued audiences' curiosity enough to become a cult classic, though it never reached the heights of *The Exorcist* or, two years later, *The Omen*, a story of the Antichrist coming to Earth in the form of a little boy born of a jackal. Adopted by an American ambassador (the legendary Gregory Peck), the child, known as Damien, ends up wreaking havoc and killing all those around him. This, too, was a box-office smash. And just like that, a genre was reborn.

A series of supernatural successes soon followed (see "Paranormal Phenomena," page 82), with out-of-the-ordinary thrillers attracting millions of fans to theaters worldwide.

(see "Paranormal Phenomena," page 82)

WILLIAM FRIEDKIN
DIRECTS LINDA BLAIR
IN *THE EXORCIST*
1973

"IT WASN'T JUST ABOUT SCARING PEOPLE, IT WAS A FAMILY DRAMA THAT HAD HORRIFIC ELEMENTS. IT'S NOT A HORROR MOVIE."

—Linda Blair on *The Exorcist*

Audience members were shocked by 13-year-old Linda Blair's demonic antics.

81

JACK NICHOLSON, IN *THE SHINING* 1980

PARANORMAL PHENOMENA

The '70s and '80s saw their fair share of otherwordly horror thrillers.

Carrie | 1976
Terrorized by classmates and her mother, a telekinetic high schooler (Sissy Spacek) turns the tables.

Damien: Omen II | 1978
An adolescent Damien terrorizes new family members and those unlucky enough to be nearby.

The Amityville Horror | 1979
A family is terrorized by a haunted house; supposedly based on a true story (see "Real-Life Haunted Houses," page 85).

Phantasm | 1979
A group of teens is terrorized by a mysterious gravedigger with a devastating arsenal of weapons.

The Fog | 1980
A deep fog and a ghostly pirate ship terrorize San Francisco in John Carpenter's film.

The Changeling | 1980
A man who watched his family die in a car crash is terrorized by a specter at home.

The Shining | 1980
Jack Nicholson stars as an author taking care of a haunted hotel who is slowly driven mad by the ghosts living there.

From the author of CARRIE,
THE SHINING,
THE DEAD ZONE,
and CHRISTINE...

An adult
nightmare.

Stephen King's
CHILDREN OF THE CORN
And a child shall lead them...

ANGEL HEART
1987

CHUCKY, IN
CHILD'S PLAY
1988

This rising tide of supernatural horror led to 1982's *Poltergeist*, in which a family finds its new California home terrorized by vengeful ghosts, only to discover that the house is built atop an old graveyard. The headstones were removed, *but not the bodies!* The biggest horror hit since *The Exorcist*, *Poltergeist* was directed by *The Texas Chainsaw Massacre*'s Tobe Hooper—with help from Steven Spielberg, who conceived the story and *might* have directed a good deal of it.

That was an early peak, followed by surprisingly few other examples. There was the Stephen King novel adaptation *Children of the Corn* in 1984, and in 1987 came the noir-esque *Angel Heart*, with Mickey Rourke, Lisa Bonet and Robert De Niro. Then horror auteur Clive Barker kicked off his *Hellraiser* series and introduced the character Pinhead. A year later came *Child's Play*, which gave the world the indomitable Chucky, an entity that would inspire numerous sequels and become one of horror's most abiding personalities and inspirations.

Speaking of Chucky, is anything creepier than a possessed doll? The vacant eyes, waxy skin and garish coloring, harnessed by an evil spirit, go way back in movies and even TV. Whether toys or ventriloquists' props, dolls have an eerie capacity for terror. In 1963, *The Twilight Zone*'s "Living Doll" episode creeped out TV viewers, and the movie *Devil Doll* picked up the thread in 1964. After Chucky, *The Puppet Master* series gave us Blade; next came Annabelle, doll star of *The Conjuring, Annabelle* and the most recent entry, 2019's *Annabelle Comes Home*.

Throughout these years, witch movies kept trickling out. Just as a talking doll can freak you out, a normal-looking, or even attractive, person with supernatural powers is also deeply unsettling. Unlike a lot of horror, witch stories are often treated with humor—think TV's *Bewitched* and movies like *The Witches of Eastwick* and *Hocus Pocus*. But witches star in much darker tales as well, like Italian director Dario Argento's 1977 thriller *Suspiria*, the 1996 teen witch flick *The Craft* or the 2016 indie flick *The Witch*. Covens, you see, are always worth watching.

Despite a fairly steady flow of supernatural horror movies in the century's last decade, the subgenre was starting to flag. But in the late 1990s, it got two big shots in the arm. First, a rash of extremely eerie Japanese movies were big international hits, warranting American remakes. Films like *The Ring*, *The Grudge*, *Dark Water* and *One Missed Call* all scored big in

LIZZIE BORDEN HOUSE

MANSON HOUSE

VILLISCA HOUSE

AMITYVILLE HORROR HOUSE

JAMES BROLIN　MARGOT KIDDER　ROD STEIGER

THE AMITYVILLE HORROR

FOR GOD'S SAKE, GET OUT!

REAL-LIFE HAUNTED HOUSES

Want to live with something really scary? Try taking up residence at a home where a bloody murder has taken place. Here, a few of the more famous abodes that have seen their share of slaughter.

Amityville Horror House This Long Island, New York, house is where Ronald J. DeFeo Jr. murdered his family in 1974. The next occupants said it was haunted, and though their claims were debunked, 1979's *The Amityville Horror* was a big hit playing off the fright.

Lizzie Borden Home This Fall River, Massachusetts, home is where Lizzie Borden famously took an ax and gave her (step)mother 40 whacks. (And then, as the rhyme goes, she gave her father 41.) More than 125 years after Borden was tried and acquitted of the murders, the house is now a bed-and-breakfast where you can spend the night amid the ghosts.

Manson House A once-glamorous Hollywood home turned into a bloody murder scene after Charles Manson and his followers slaughtered

five people in 1969, including pregnant actress Sharon Tate. The home was razed in 1994 and rebuilt with a new address, but neighbors report ghostly apparitions still occasionally drop by.

Villisca House On a quiet spring night in 1912, six family members plus two young houseguests were brutally massacred in their beds by an ax murderer in the rural hamlet of Villisca, Iowa. The killer was never found. The humble old white frame house is now a creepy B and B, where guests brave paranormal interactions.

the U.S. Then, in 1999, filmmaker M. Night Shyamalan gave us *The Sixth Sense*, and nothing was ever the same.

Shyamalan's tale of a young boy who sees dead people continues to be not only one of the highest-grossing horror films of all time, but also one of the highest-grossing movies, period. The thriller kept audiences guessing until the film's final minutes, establishing horror's legitimacy as a genre worth taking seriously—and talking about, a lot. The relatively gore-free movie earned six Oscar nominations, including Best Picture, and made Shyamalan a star.

In the 20-plus years since that release, supernatural horror has come roaring back. *The Blair Witch Project* exploded onto the scene in 1999, blowing people's minds at the Sundance Film Festival and making almost a quarter-billion dollars worldwide on a budget of just $60,000. It also launched the found-footage style of storytelling that propelled another ultra-low-budget hit, *Paranormal Activity*, in 2007. Five sequels followed. *The Others*

(2001), starring Nicole Kidman, was greatly influenced by *The Innocents*, while offerings like *Sinister* and *The Conjuring* spawned franchises of their own.

Other popular supernatural titles include *The Babadook*, *Mama*, *Oculus*, *Orphan* and *Drag Me to Hell*, and in 2018, there was *Hereditary*, a flick from the *Rosemary's Baby* school of demonic existence. The movie did solid, if unspectacular, business. A blip, really, on the terrifying ghost train—but a part of a genre that isn't likely to fade away. ￭

HALEY JOEL OSMENT, IN *THE SIXTH SENSE* 1999

M. NIGHT SHYAMALAN

MILLY SHAPIRO, IN *HEREDITARY* 2018

VERA FARMIGA, IN *THE CONJURING* 2013

SISSY SPACEK,
IN *CARRIE*
1976

87

07

ALIEN, 1979

INVADERS FROM MARS, 1953

SCIENCE FICTION

SCI-FI
TO DIE FOR
ALIENS KILL US. TECHNOLOGY FAILS US. HOW THE SCARIEST FORM OF HORROR MANIFESTS OUR MODERN ANXIETIES.

Science is at the heart of so much horror. Victor Frankenstein tries to re-create life. Archaeologists dig up an ancient mummy. A lab-grown virus triggers a zombie outbreak. As our reliance on science has grown, so has our fear of it. Now that technology pervades every aspect of our lives, horror based on science fiction is also everywhere.

Frankenstein aside, science fiction–based horror really took off in the 1950s, a decade gripped by anxieties about nuclear war, automation and our earliest forays into space. Many great sci-fi horror movies involve aliens and technology, as well as body-switching—sometimes all at once.

The 1951 classic *The Thing From Another World* has been remade several times, never better

than as 1982's *The Thing* by John Carpenter. This story of an alien entity that inhabits bodies of living mammals and uses them to invade an Antarctic research station is a perfect example of the genre, as it deals with all three at once.

Same with the various incarnations of *Invaders From Mars*, which was first made in 1953 and, in the words of a man born in 1943 (who happens to be the father of one of this book's editors), "scared the ever-living hell out of me. I still can't watch it." That's the kind of thing that makes good horror, no matter what the era.

Sci-fi horror may reach far into the future, or it may imagine a different present, home to either extraterrestrials or different technology. It also makes for fantastic social commentary. The

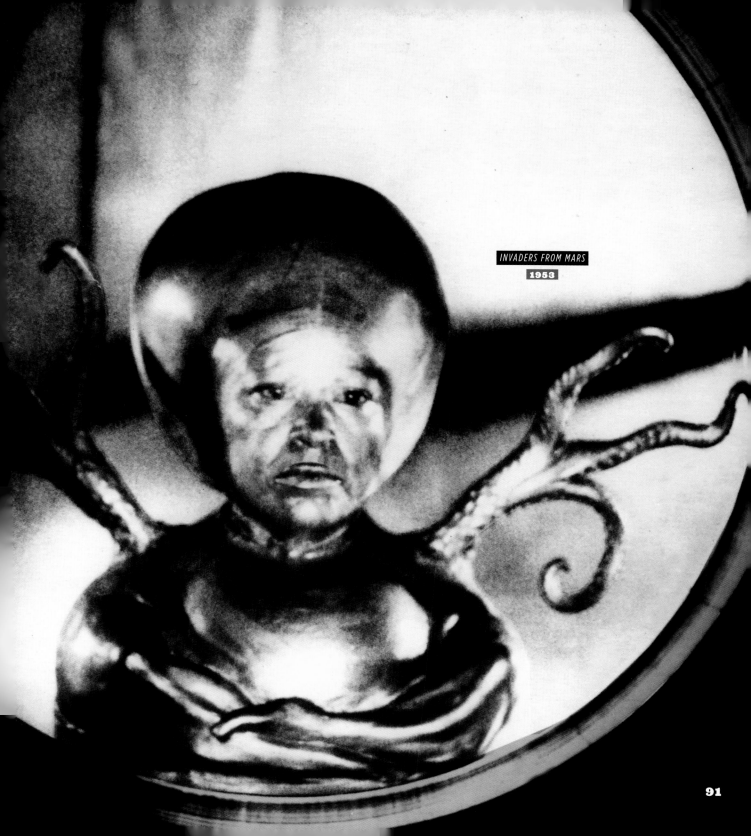

INVADERS FROM MARS
1953

1956 classic *Invasion of the Body Snatchers* is a perfect allegory for the McCarthyism that had swept the U.S. in the first half of the decade. The 1978 remake, starring Donald Sutherland and Leonard Nimoy, doesn't have quite the same resonance. Same with another John Carpenter film 32 years later: *They Live*, starring professional wrestler Rowdy Roddy Piper—featuring the epic line, "I have come here to chew

bubble gum and kick ass. And I'm all out of bubble gum"—is a pitch-perfect commentary on 1980s consumerism. Another much-lauded example of horror as social commentary, 2017's *Get Out*, is based on a preposterous scientific procedure.

Two things—action and imagery—set this genre apart from the rest of horror. The focus on technology and aliens drives bigger, faster-paced sequences.

Take, for instance, the *Alien* franchise. Director Ridley Scott's 1979 original is a standard one-location tale with a bunch of overmatched people being stalked by an unbeatable creature. The scene where the infant alien bursts forth from actor John Hurt's chest (see sidebar, page 96), is one of the most famous in movie history. *Aliens*, the 1986 sequel directed by John Cameron, is not just terrifying; it's one

KEVIN McCARTHY AND DANA WYNTER, IN *INVASION OF THE BODY SNATCHERS* **1956**

THE THING **1982**

JAMES ARNESS, IN *THE THING FROM ANOTHER WORLD* **1951**

"JUST BECAUSE YOU'RE MAKING A HORROR FILM DOESN'T MEAN YOU CAN'T MAKE AN ARTFUL FILM."
—David Cronenberg

JULIAN RICHINGS, IN *CUBE*
1997

JEFF GOLDBLUM, IN *THE FLY*
1986

THE BROOD
1979

CLOVERFIELD
2008

VIN DIESEL,
IN *THE CHRONICLES
OF RIDDICK*
2004

of the decade's finest action flicks. Though two more sequels disappointed creatively and financially, the franchise returned to life in 2012 with *Prometheus* and then, five years later, *Alien: Covenant*, which explored the genesis of the iconic creatures.

As for imagery, sci-fi horror flicks often shock audiences with gore and radical visual effects. Canadian filmmaker David Cronenberg is probably the most visionary sci-fi horror director. Between 1977 and 1983, he pushed boundaries with exploding heads, weird human-technology interactions and other extreme images in movies like *Rabid*, *The Brood*, *Scanners* and *Videodrome*. His 1986 remake of the 1950s schlockfest *The Fly* stars Jeff Goldblum as a scientist who accidentally turns himself into a human-size version of the household pest. As the transformation continues, Goldblum's character becomes more and more grotesque.

Many movies, like these two from 1997, follow in Cronenberg's footsteps without the same panache. In *Cube*, a group is thrown into a mysterious, ever-shifting series of rooms, each a total deathtrap. The worst death? Invisible wires that literally dice the victim into dozens of tiny pieces. In *Event Horizon*, a spaceship goes through an interdimensional portal and

There are 4 billion people on earth.
237 are Scanners.
They have the most terrifying powers ever created
...and they are winning.

10 SECONDS.
The Pain Begins.

15 SECONDS.
You Can't Breathe.

20 SECONDS.
You Explode.

SCANNERS
...Their thoughts can kill!

EVENT HORIZON
1997

PREDATOR
2017

JESSE PLEMONS, IN
BLACK MIRROR
2017

95

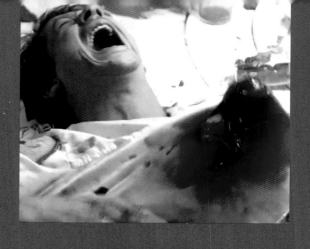

returns with a literal piece of hell that drives victims to pluck out their own eyes and hold them in their hands. A year later, in Robert Rodriguez's *The Faculty*, slithery aliens invade the bodies of high school teachers; one decapitated victim's head crawls back to its body and reattaches itself. Such images tend to linger.

Some sci-fi horror ends up being fairly mainstream, replete with big action scenes and big box office. Arnold Schwarzenegger's 1987 action epic *Predator* and its sequels are good examples, as are producer J. J. Abrams' *Cloverfield* films, which involve massive alien invasions. Vin Diesel's space-set Riddick trilogy, which begins with the 2000 film *Pitch Black*, is another great example. All these series were big hits. In fact, director Shane Black's *The Predator* sequel did solid business as recently as September 2018.

As technology creeps into every crevice of our lives, sci-fi horror continues to explore the human-tech interface. Netflix's *Black Mirror* anthology series is generally bloodless yet awesomely terrifying, precisely because its alternate—or worse, imminent—realities seem so very possible, even likely. At its most effective, sci-fi horror holds up a dark mirror to modern science and shows how it may eventually be the end of us all. And that's what makes it so scary. ◾

WHY THAT SCENE IN *ALIEN* FREAKS YOU OUT

It's one of the most famous scenes in movies, and for good reason: Nothing like it had ever been seen before. As a group of miners on a spaceship sits at dinner, one goes into convulsions and then falls onto the table. Suddenly, an alien being bursts from his chest. Actor John Hurt, who died in 2017 at age 77, knew how pivotal a scene it was. He even spoofed it at the end of Mel Brooks' 1987 comedy, *Spaceballs*, in which an alien bursts from his chest. He sighs, "Oh, no. Not again."

The original sequence is very simple. It comes after Hurt's character, Kane, has been implanted with an alien embryo. When the alien becomes viable, it erupts from within, killing him in the process. One reason the scene works so well is how the other characters respond. The actors—including Sigourney Weaver, Tom Skerritt, Yaphet Kotto, Ian Holm, Harry Dean Stanton and Veronica Cartwright—didn't know what was going to happen. "All it said in the script was, 'This thing emerges,'" Weaver said in a 1979 interview with *Empire* magazine.

The day that scene was shot, director Ridley Scott isolated Hurt from his castmates, then brought them all together on set without telling them what was happening. When the alien emerged, Cartwright passed out. "Oh man! It was real, man," Kotto told *Empire*. "We didn't see that coming. We were freaked. The actors were all frightened. And Veronica nutted out." Almost four decades later, it's still one of the craziest, scariest, most incredible scenes on film.

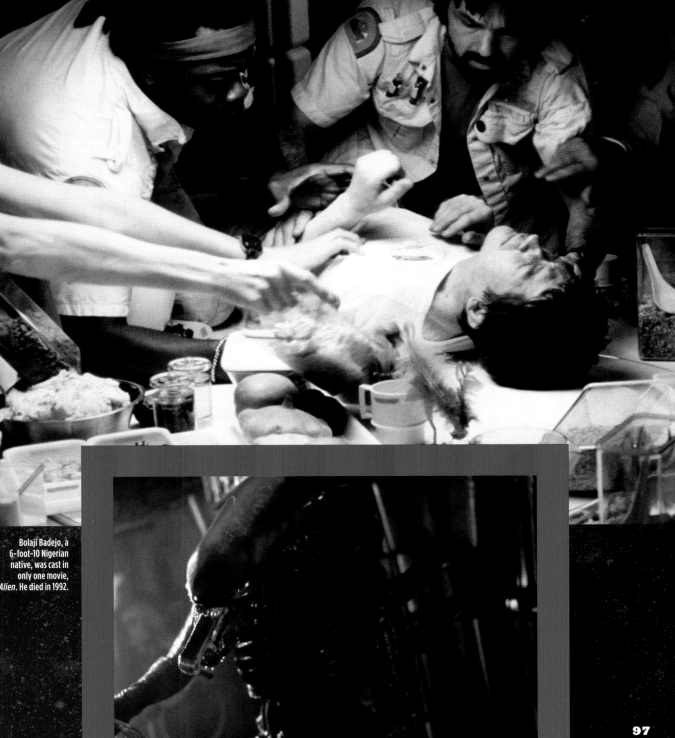

Bolaji Badejo, a 6-foot-10 Nigerian native, was cast in only one movie, *Alien*. He died in 1992.

08

HALLOWEEN, 1978

SLASHERS

PSYCHO, 1960

NOTHING LIKE THE
REAL THING

THE SCARIEST MONSTERS ARE THE ONES WHO LOOK LIKE YOUR NEXT-DOOR NEIGHBOR: WHY WE LOVE SLASHER MOVIES.

Demons, devils and the reanimated or living dead; strange beasts roaming the countryside; ghouls, goblins and mysterious entities that go kill in the night—they're all frightening, in their own terrible way, but they can also be dismissed. You can reason away that kind of scare by reassuring yourself: *It's OK! It's not real!*

But some monsters don't go away so easily. Some fiends are terrifying because they really could be...real. They're deranged villains who don't just threaten harm in the fiction of film, TV, books and nightmares but who knock on your door and bring the terror straight to you. Sometimes they don't even bother to knock.

That's why characters like Michael Myers, Jason Voorhees, Freddy Krueger, Norman Bates and Thomas Brown Hewitt (aka Leatherface) are so successful. It's

the real-life monsters, even those who might be touched by a bit of the supernatural or superhuman, who really get under your skin. *Deep* under your skin.

Slasher films have been around for longer than you might think. Their roots lie in things as innocent as Agatha Christie novels and Sherlock Holmes stories. Alfred Hitchcock's *Psycho* and Michael Powell's *Peeping Tom*, both of which were released in 1960, were the first true examples of the genre. Their successes inspired knockoffs from Britain's Hammer Film Productions and American exploitation king Roger Corman's American International Pictures. They also sparked a slew of Italian gorefests, called *giallo* films, that redefined what horror movies could be. (*Giallo*, Italian for yellow, referred to the covers of early pulp paperbacks.)

Brad Loree's Michael Myers closes in on Jamie Lee Curtis' Laurie Strode in 2002's *Halloween: Resurrection.* (This moment was erased from continuity with the release of the 2018 *Halloween.*)

The genre also jump-started the career of *Godfather* auteur Francis Ford Coppola, who made *Dementia 13* for Corman in 1963. It led to the rise of gritty filmmakers like Wes Craven, who exploded onto the scene in 1972 with *Last House on the Left*, about a gang of criminals that rapes and murders two teenage girls, then terrorizes the family of one of them while hiding out from the law. The film cost just $87,000 to make (less than $525,000 in today's dollars) and grossed more than $3 million ($18 million today). These movies paved the way for the real breakthrough: Tobe Hooper's 1974 masterpiece, *The Texas Chain Saw Massacre*, which cost roughly $300,000 to make but reaped more than 100 times that at movie theaters.

Clearly, a pattern had emerged: Make a scary movie with human monsters as the murderous villains, spend next to nothing on the production, and watch the money roll in. Just as *Psycho*'s villainous Norman Bates gave birth to *Chainsaw Massacre*'s Leatherface, he also begat Michael Myers, the psychopathic killer who terrorized teens in John Carpenter's 1978 classic, *Halloween*.

That film's genius lay not just in how scary it was—spoiler alert: It's really, really scary—but in how it took the basic tenets of the genre

Robbi Morgan is totally on edge in the 1980 classic *Friday the 13th.*

NED BELLAMY, IN *SAW* 2004

ANTHONY PERKINS, IN *PSYCHO* 1960

"I WENT HOME, SAT DOWN, ALL THE CHANNELS JUST TUNED IN, THE ZEITGEIST BLEW THROUGH, AND THE WHOLE DAMN STORY CAME TO ME IN WHAT SEEMED LIKE ABOUT THIRTY SECONDS."

—*Texas Chain Saw Massacre* director Tobe Hooper

CHUCKY, IN
SEED OF CHUCKY
2005

Murderer and rapist Krug Stillo, played by David Hess, gets his just desserts in 1972's *The Last House on the Left*.

and ran with them, essentially creating a new paradigm for films that would follow. It took the general concept of the Last Girl—a young woman left alone to face the killer at the movie's climax—to the next level with the introduction of Jamie Lee Curtis' Laurie Strode. Not only did the movie make the daughter of Tony Curtis and Janet Leigh a star—and one of the great Scream Queens—it solidified a format that dozens would follow.

It also did one other thing: It began what is considered the golden age of slasher movies, an era that gave us *Friday the 13th, When a Stranger Calls, Prom Night, Terror Train* and *The Fog* (Curtis appeared in the last three of these), *Dressed to Kill, My Bloody Valentine, The Burning, A Nightmare on Elm Street* and sequels to both *Halloween* and

Friday the 13th (in the latter's case, three of them), among many others—all released between the years 1978 and 1984.

In each of those films, the basic premise was the same: A psycho killer on the loose, hunting unsuspecting victims. Over the next 10 years, the so-called silver age took hold, with more *Friday the 13th, Halloween, Elm Street* and *Chainsaw Massacre* sequels, as well as new franchises like *Child's Play* and *The Stepfather*—each of which gave audiences new villains to hate and fear. None of the new films broke the same kind of ground the golden age films had, but they did employ the tropes those earlier films had established. Unfortunately, that also meant driving some of them into the ground and bringing about "slasher fatigue," which led

the major franchises' popularity to fade away for a bit.

Then came *Scream*. Amazingly, the thing that infused the most energy back into slasher films was perhaps the greatest satire of them ever made, by a director who had helped create the genre. Craven's 1995 smash hit not only made fun of the genre in the most meta way possible, but it was a genuinely scary horror flick. Nine years before *Shaun of the Dead* did the same for zombie films, *Scream* set an incredibly high standard: If you were going to make fun of something, fans said as they flocked to multiplexes, you'd better bring your A game.

Scream did two things. It ushered in an age of films satirizing various genres by pointing out the genre's tropes while also employing them. It also began a new era of slasher film that included *I Know What You Did Last Summer*, *Urban Legend*, *Jeepers Creepers*, *Wrong Turn* and several sequels of older franchises, like *Halloween*, *Friday the 13th* and *Nightmare on Elm Street*. Of course, *Scream* itself became a franchise.

Soon after the turn of the century, the slasher genre gave rise to a subgenre called "torture porn," which, as the name suggests, involves elaborate scenes of torture. This term was applied to the 2005 Eli Roth film *Hostel* and also to films like James Wan's low-budget sensation, *Saw*, as well as *The Devil's Rejects* and *Wolf Creek*, among others. It's worth noting that the creators of the *Saw* franchise rejected the "torture porn" moniker.

That fad came and went, and more recent slasher films, like *The Cabin in the Woods* and *Tucker & Dale vs. Evil*, tend toward more self-awareness about the genre itself and its overall effect on audiences.

And the slasher genre is still very much alive. From the rebooted *Halloween 2018* (once again starring Jamie Lee Curtis) to the anticipated 2020 release of, yes, *Halloween Kills* (more of the same), it's clear our appetite for cheap thrills has not yet abated. ▬

GHOSTFACE, IN *SCREAM 4* 2011

Jennifer Lim faces torture as Kana in 2005's grisly *Hostel*.

JASON VOORHEES, IN *FRIDAY THE 13TH PART VIII: JASON TAKES MANHATTAN* 1989

ANNABELLE, IN *THE CONJURING* 2013

Robert Englund, in the movie that made him famous as Freddy Krueger: 1984's *A Nightmare on Elm Street.*

"HORROR DOES BETTER WHEN IT'S BUBBLING UNDER. IT'S A NICHE. IT DOESN'T LIKE THE LIMELIGHT."

—Robert Englund

SCREAM QUEENS

WHAT BECOMES A LEGEND MOST?
A TOUGH WOMAN WHO SURVIVES A TERRIFYING
ENCOUNTER WITH A BLOODTHIRSTY KILLER,
AGAIN AND AGAIN AND AGAIN AND AGAIN AND
AGAIN AND AGAIN AND AGAIN. AND AGAIN.

Some got naked and died; some stayed virginal and survived. Every now and again, one would sneak through with a little sex but still escape. Of the greatest Scream Queens in movie history, a select few left the genre, while others reveled in their status as horror royalty. What they all have in common is the ability to scare, be scared and, most importantly, kick serious ass when needed. Many become the Last Girl: that sole survivor who escapes alive, however bloody and disheveled.

The list of actresses who have led horror flicks is long and full of stars. Plenty—like Fay Wray, in the original *King Kong*, or Sissy Spacek in *Carrie*—appeared in a single, great horror flick. But to make this list, an actress must have appeared in at least two features. It's why TV actresses, like *The Walking Dead*'s Lauren

Cohan, don't make the list. Likewise, though an impressive array of scream queens thrive in ultra-low-budget and straight-to-video projects—Tristan Risk, Agnes Bruckner and Lauren Ashley Carter come to mind— we're sticking to the mainstream. Here's a look at our top shriekers.

10

JANET LEIGH

But wait! Didn't she only have that one, iconic role in *Psycho*? In fact, Leigh not only appeared with daughter Jamie Lee Curtis in *The Fog*, she also showed up—complete with her 1957 Ford Custom 300 Fordor sedan—in *Halloween H20: 20 Years Later*, again opposite Jamie Lee. Before she starred in Hitchcock's landmark 1960 film, she had been a Hollywood stalwart for years, perhaps best known for Orson Welles' ill-fated 1958 classic, *Touch of Evil*. After *Psycho*, her biggest role was opposite Frank Sinatra in *The Manchurian Candidate* (1962) before she scaled back her acting career and worked sporadically until her death in 2004.

After filming the murder sequence in *Psycho*, Janet Leigh never took another shower.

Jane Levy, seen here in *Evil Dead*, was best known for the sitcom *Suburgatory* before becoming a certified Scream Queen.

9
JANE LEVY

This relative newcomer's work in just the past decade qualifies her. First there was her role in *Evil Dead*, the 2013 remake of the 1981 horror classic. Whereas Sam Raimi's original—indeed, his whole trilogy—masterfully combined comedy and horror, the remake was all about the latter, with Levy as Mia, the Last Girl. Surviving that rural massacre, she ended up in a more urban setting for *Don't Breathe*, a low-budget 2016 joint that followed three amateur burglars who try to rip off a blind man but it goes—all together now—*horribly wrong*. The movie was a stunning smash and cemented Levy's horror cred. She returned to the genre in 2018 in Hulu's horror series *Castle Rock*, based on stories by Stephen King.

MARILYN BURNS

Just as *The Texas Chain Saw Massacre* kick-started the wave of 1970s slasher films, Marilyn Burns became a trailblazer for her role as Sally Hardesty, the movie's female lead and survivor. Through the years, Burns did some mainstream work, like the 1976 TV movie about the Manson family, *Helter Skelter*. She also had a lead role in the frat-boy gorefest *Future Kill* (1985), but she repeatedly returned to the franchise that made her a cult hero. She worked again with director Tobe Hooper in *Eaten Alive* (1976) and later had cameos in *Texas Chainsaw Massacre: The Next Generation* (1995) and *Texas Chainsaw 3D* (2013). Burns died in her sleep on August 5, 2014, at the age of 65.

Her work in
the *Chainsaw*
movies defined
Burns' career.

7 BARBARA STEELE

Most Scream Queens are American, but that's more of a guideline than a rule, as is proven by British actress Barbara Steele. This raven-haired beauty made her horror debut in Mario Bava's 1960 thriller *Black Sunday* and then starred in a string of scary movies that solidified her status. Over just the next decade, she was in Roger Corman's adaptation of Poe's *The Pit and the Pendulum* plus *The Horrible Dr. Hitchcock*, *The Ghost*, *Castle of Blood*, *The Long Hair of Death*, *Terror-Creatures From the Grave*, *Nightmare Castle*, *The She-Beast* and *The Crimson Cult* (with Boris Karloff and Christopher Lee). In 1964 alone, she appeared in eight films (not all horror). Steele later branched out into producing, even winning an Emmy for the 1988 miniseries *War and Remembrance*, but she has never stopped acting. She was in the 1991 remake of the vampire soap opera *Dark Shadows* and acted as recently as 2016, in the horror anthology *Minutes Past Midnight*.

6

Among our Scream Queens, only Langenkamp can claim fame from a single franchise. Known for three different *A Nightmare on Elm Street* films, two of them directed by the late Wes Craven, she had a small cameo in Craven's *Shocker*, as "Victim." She appeared as Nancy Thompson in the first *Elm Street* movie and in 1987's *A Nightmare on Elm Street 3: Dream Warriors*. In 1994, when Craven returned to the franchise he'd started, with *Wes Craven's New Nightmare*, his meta story had Langenkamp playing a fictionalized version of herself. With Freddy Krueger back in action, the actress had to return to the role that made her famous, just to stop him. Craven also appeared, as did Robert Englund, who played both himself and Freddy. Langenkamp is still active as a TV and film actress, but she and her husband also own and run AFX Studio, which has won awards for its makeup work in both film and TV.

Talk about speaking in tongues! Heather Langenkamp takes an obscene call in *Nightmare*.

"I DO WISH I'D HAD A BETTER CAREER. WHO WOULDN'T?"
—Heather Langenkamp

5

SARAH MICHELLE GELLAR

Seven years on TV as iconic vampire hunter Buffy Summers would probably be enough to establish Sarah Michelle Gellar's bona fides, but that's just part of her horror résumé. One year after she first ventured to Sunnyvale (and the Hell Mouth on which it sat), Gellar starred in *I Know What You Did Last Summer*, opposite her future husband, Freddie Prinze Jr., and Jennifer Love Hewitt. That staple of 1990s teen horror boosted her fame and horror cred to new levels—and then she was in *Scream 2* that same year. After a pair of *Scooby-Doo* movies, also with Prinze, she starred in the American remake of the Japanese horror flick *Ju-On: The Grudge*. The U.S. version, *The Grudge*, was a monster hit in 2004, grossing $187 million worldwide on a $10 million budget. The 2006 sequel wasn't as successful, but it kept Gellar in the game. She has since appeared in such titles as *The Return* and *Possession*, and she stays busy in both horror and mainstream fare.

4

LINDA BLAIR

...en your first-ever starring role leads to an
...ar nomination for Best Supporting Actress,
...'s hard to top. Linda Blair's Regan MacNeil
...some pretty horrific things in 1973's
...*Exorcist*, spinning her head completely
...und and vomiting green slime onto a
...of priests, so maybe the Academy was
...aid of what would happen if they *didn't*
...minate her. In the years since, while Blair
...n't reached similar heights as an actress,
...'s continued to thrill audiences in a series
...orror flicks, including the 1977 sequel,
...*rcist II: The Heretic*, as well as *Hell Night*,
...*tesque*, *The Chilling* and plenty more.
..., it's Regan MacNeil who leaves the
...gest impression. Obviously, you can't
...sturbate with a crucifix while spouting
...anic curses without making a mark on the
...ure. It's one thing to be in what may be
...scariest movie of all time. It's another
...g to be the scariest part of that movie.

Don't let the makeup fool you: Linda Blair
was actually a sweet 13-year-old girl
when she made *The Exorcist*

NEVE CAMPBELL

Neve Campbell was a known quantity when she starred as Sidney Prescott in Wes Craven's 1996 horror satire, *Scream*. She'd come to fame on the Fox drama *Party of Five*, but she'd already established her horror cred earlier that year in the teen witch flick *The Craft*. That movie, in which four outcasts form a coven (with predictably disastrous results), hit theaters that May. But it was *Scream*, released five days before Christmas, that would cement her queenly status. *Scream* doubled as both a satire of the genre and a perfect example of it, anchored by Campbell's star turn as the Last Girl. Campbell's Sidney has appeared in all three sequels, including *Scream 4* in 2011 (she's also rumored to be in 2021's *Scream 5*). She continues to work regularly, appearing on such shows as *Grey's Anatomy* and *House of Cards* and playing Dwayne "The Rock" Johnson's wife in the 2018 blockbuster *Skyscraper*.

2

DANIELLE HARRIS

Few women become Scream Queens before they've even turned 13, but Danielle Harris entered the pantheon even earlier. She was only 11 when she starred in the 1988 sequel *Halloween 4: The Return of Michael Myers* and just a year older in *Halloween 5: The Revenge of Michael Myers*. She's the only actress from the original Halloween series to be cast in Rob Zombie's 2007 remake. As Laurie Strode's best friend, Annie Brackett, she survived the first Zombie effort and made it to the 2009 sequel (unlike the Annie of John Carpenter's 1978 original, who met a bloody end). In between her *Halloween* outings, Harris appeared in the 1998 flick *Urban Legend* and has been a horror regular in movies like *Stake Land*, *Hallow's Eve* and *Havenhurst*, to name a few. She took over the lead role in the Hatchet series, for *Hatchet II*, *Hatchet III* and *Victor Crowley*, and was in Quentin Tarantino's *Once Upon a Time...in Hollywood*.

1 JAMIE LEE CURTIS

Not the first Scream Queen and not the last—but most definitely the very best. After debuting as Laurie Strode in 1978's *Halloween*, Jamie Lee Curtis would star over the next four years in *Prom Night*, *The Fog*, *Terror Train*, *Road Games* and *Halloween II*. For many, that would be an entire career. For Jamie Lee, it was just the start. The talented daughter of actors Tony Curtis and Janet Leigh, she soon branched out into mainstream fare, like *Trading Places*, *A Fish Called Wanda* and *True Lies*, becoming a genuine movie star and an incredibly capable comedic actress.

It wasn't until the 1998 sequel, *Halloween H20: 20 Years Later*, that she returned to the genre that first made her. Playing a grown-up Laurie Strode (who's been living under an alias since her brother, Michael Myers, went berserk and killed a whole bunch of people), she has a surprisingly moving and poignant moment with him before cutting his head off right at the film's climax. Four years later, in an odd (and, to many, unnecessary) sequel, *Halloween: Resurrection*, she finally dies at her brother's hand.

One might have thought this would end her horror career. But in 2015, she joined the Fox comedy-horror hybrid series *Scream Queens*, playing the dean of a college where a serial killer has begun taking out coeds. It was perfect casting, and she dug into the role with relish, giving a winking performance that made it clear she was having a lot of fun being back in this particular sandbox. So much fun, in fact, that she signed on once again to play Laurie Strode in the reboot *Halloween:2018* and will appear in 2021's *Halloween Ends*. Fans will be lining up around the block to see it—and, most especially, her. ▬

"WE WERE MAKING AN EXPLOITATION SLASHER MOVIE ABOUT KILLING BABYSITTERS. AND THAT'S WHAT IT WAS... IT BECAME THE THING YOU COULD GET ANOTHER JOB FROM, NOT THAT IT WAS GOING TO BECOME SOMETHING."

—Jamie Lee Curtis on underestimating *Halloween*

69

THE TEXAS CHAIN SAW MASSACRE, 1974

MEMORABLE MOVIES

TERROR'S TOP 13

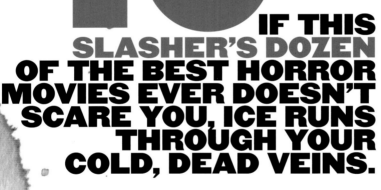

IF THIS SLASHER'S DOZEN OF THE BEST HORROR MOVIES EVER DOESN'T SCARE YOU, ICE RUNS THROUGH YOUR COLD, DEAD VEINS.

SIGOURNEY WEAVER

Any ranking of greatest films ever is going to get some folks riled up—after all, a best-of list is a collection of opinions, not facts. Even taking that into account, it's hard to argue with the list we've assembled.

How'd we do it? We looked at 100 years of horror movies and picked the best. Between the 13 that made the list and the 20 honorable mentions, they cover an enormous amount of ground, addressing different subgenres and types of terror. It's important to note that at least a couple of titles won extra points for how groundbreaking they were, particularly numbers 12 and 9. Inevitably, some personal favorites didn't make the cut—*sorry!*—but each of these movies undeniably represents a major event in the history of horror. ◼

13.
ALIEN

1979 It's one of the best taglines in movie history: "In space, no one can hear you scream." Director Ridley Scott did something no one had ever successfully done before. He took the monster movie into deep space, using the standard structure of a one-location story and turning it into something else entirely. Miners traveling through space get a distress call and divert course to check it out. They find an enormous desiccated alien corpse surrounded by what look like oversize eggs. When one of the miners comes face-to-face with one of the eggs, the horror really begins.

If the movie had only made Sigourney Weaver a star, that would have been enough—but it also took the concept of a slasher movie and set it in a place with literally no escape. The alien hunts down each crew member as part of its own evolutionary reason for existence. The introduction of an android working at cross-purposes with its human counterparts only heightens the terror. On top of all that, the movie also pulls off the rare trick of being a true science fiction film that portrays space travel and the reasons for it as realistic and unspectacular. What remains spectacular, however, is the danger that lurks in the great beyond.

PolyGram Pictures presents a Lycanthrope Films Limited production
An American Werewolf in London
starring David Naughton, Jenny Agutter, Griffin Dunne & John Woodvine
Original music by Elmer Bernstein · Executive producers Peter Guber & Jon Peters
Produced by George Folsey, Jr. · Written and directed by John Landis

PolyGram Pictures

"Meco's Impressions of An American Werewolf in London"
Marketed by PolyGram Records

© 1981 PolyGram Pictures, Ltd.

A NAZI DEMON IN
DAVID'S NIGHTMARE

GRIFFIN DUNNE

DAVID NAUGHTON

12.
AN AMERICAN WEREWOLF IN LONDON

1981 Just as *Alien* doubles as a sci-fi film, *An American Werewolf in London* comes off as a comedy; a dark, disturbing, ultraviolent and exceedingly gory comedy, but a comedy nonetheless. Young American David (David Naughton) and his buddy Jack (Griffin Dunne) are traipsing through the English countryside when an animal attacks them, killing Jack and badly injuring David. Soon, it becomes clear that the animal was a werewolf, and now David is one, too.

There's horror, of course, but also laugh-out-loud humor, as in the scenes where David's decaying victims come to him in visions and politely ask him to kill himself and release them from purgatory. That, combined with romance and groundbreaking special effects (it won Rick Baker the very first Oscar in that category) makes this arguably the best horror comedy in history. More than that, *An American Werewolf in London* is simply the best example of werewolf cinema ever put on the big screen.

11.
NIGHT OF THE LIVING DEAD

1968 There had been zombie movies before George Romero made his 1968 masterpiece, but none had ever put forth a proper set of zombie rules. Romero took care of that, locking a bunch of survivors in a house during a mysterious zombie uprising and then depicting everything falling apart around them. The movie is groundbreaking not just for its use of the zombie or because it defines the modern zombie (the flesh- and brain-eating undead would become canon in the decades to follow) but also because it acknowledges the contemporary civil rights movement by featuring African American actor Duane Jones in the lead role.

Night of the Living Dead loosely adapts Richard Matheson's novel *I Am Legend,* which is about the aftermath of an apocalypse caused by a virus that turns people into zombie vampires. Like other zombie movies, it isolates the victims in a single location. But when you combine its terrors with its parable/parallel about the real world— not just the civil rights movement but also Cold War paranoia and the Vietnam conflict—the movie becomes magical.

NIGHT OF THE LIVING DEAD

KYRA SCHON

SSEL W. STREINER and KARL HARDMAN Directed by GEORGE A. ROMERO Screenpl
JOEA DUANE JONES MARILYN EASTMAN KARL HARDMAN JUDITH RIDLEY KE

FROM LEFT: COURTENEY COX,
JAMIE KENNEDY
AND NEVE CAMPBELL

DREW BARRYMORE

A WES CRAVEN FILM

SCREAM

DAVID ARQUETTE   NEVE CAMPBELL   COURTENEY COX   SKEET ULRICH   AND   DREW BARRYMORE

"Scream is a Scream!"

DON'T ANSWER THE PHONE.
DON'T OPEN THE DOOR. DON'T TRY TO ESCAPE.

MIRAMAX

10. SCREAM

1996 The best satire is also an excellent example of its object, which is why *Scream* is not only one of the greatest film satires ever but also one of the greatest horror flicks. Even as it scares the holy bejeezus out of the audience, *it explains why and how it's doing just that.* Somehow, instead of being annoying, it works, applying a winning and winking sense of humor to a genuinely terrifying movie about a serial killer who's terrorizing a sleepy Northern California town.

Thanks to its director, horror legend Wes Craven, the film arrived with an impeccable pedigree already in place. But it took things a step further by introducing star Drew Barrymore in the opening scene and then (spoiler alert!) *immediately killing her off,* thus raising the stakes exponentially. By establishing that no one was safe, it threw all the horror genre's rules right out the window—while discussing in plain English what those rules actually are—or at least, what they were. In the 20-plus years since, as more and more horror flicks have employed a similar meta, self-referential style, *Scream*'s influence on the genre has only grown.

can you survive
The Texas Chain Saw Massacre
X (LONDON)
...it happened!

CAUTION
There are scenes in this film
that may be disturbing to
some members of the public

9. THE TEXAS CHAIN SAW MASSACRE

1974 It wasn't the first slasher film or even the best, but there is something deeply terrifying about it that can't be denied. Perhaps it's the cannibalistic backwoods family that terrorizes a bunch of teens. Or the villainous Leatherface, who walks around wearing a mask made of human skin. Or maybe it's that the weapon of death is *a freaking chainsaw*. You can still look at a knife or a gun without imagining a mad killer running around wreaking havoc and committing bloody murder. But a chainsaw? Good luck with that.

Director Tobe Hooper had helmed one previous feature, an experimental 1969 drama called *Eggshells*, but this more visceral film confirmed him as a horror visionary and set his career down a very specific path. This bloody, gory, pitiless movie is deeply unsettling and demands an emotional response. Some would argue that Hooper never again approached this level of filmmaking (see No. 6 on the list for further explanation), but even if that's true, who cares? He made one of the scariest movies ever. That's pretty amazing all on its own.

TERI MCMINN

GUNNAR HANSEN,
AS LEATHERFACE

131

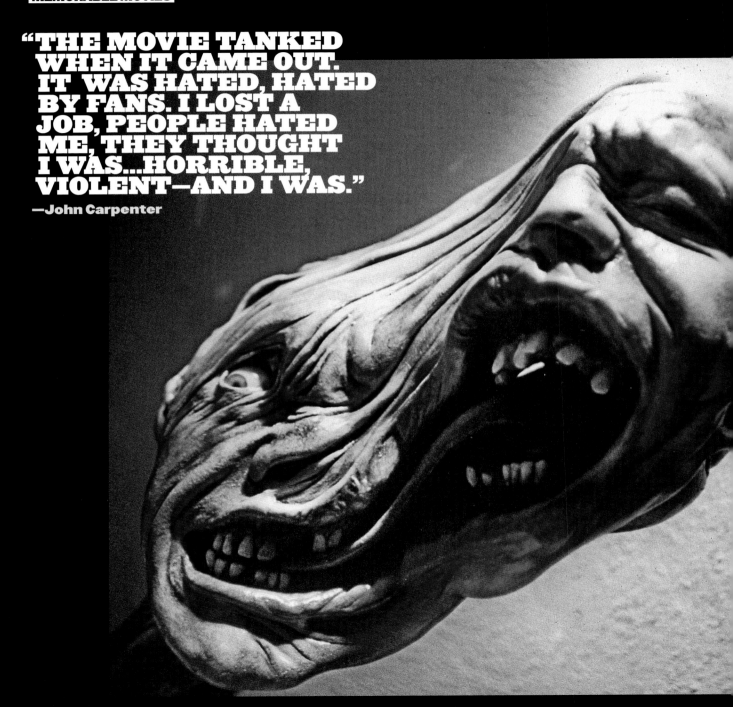

"THE MOVIE TANKED WHEN IT CAME OUT. IT WAS HATED, HATED BY FANS. I LOST A JOB, PEOPLE HATED ME, THEY THOUGHT I WAS...HORRIBLE, VIOLENT—AND I WAS."
—John Carpenter

CHARLES HALLAHAN

The ultimate in alien terror.

JOHN CARPENTER'S
THE THING

A TURMAN-FOSTER COMPANY PRODUCTION JOHN CARPENTER'S "THE THING"
KURT RUSSELL BILL LANCASTER ALBERT WHITLOCK ROB BOTTIN ENNIO MORRICONE DEAN CUNDEY LARRY FRANCO
WILBUR STARK STUART COHEN DAVID FOSTER & LAWRENCE TURMAN JOHN CARPENTER A UNIVERSAL PICTURE

8.
THE THING

1982 The only remake on this list, John Carpenter's reworking of the 1951 schlockfest *The Thing From Another World* is a tour de force of terror. Using the single-location formula, Carpenter strands a bunch of scientists—led by regular Carpenter collaborator Kurt Russell—at a remote Antarctic outpost, where they're forced to fight an alien entity that inhabits their bodies and then turns them against one another. The creature first shows up in the form of a harmless dog, and then all hell breaks loose in a genuinely terrifying series of set pieces that jacks up the paranoia and dread with each passing minute. It's almost a study in how to build tension and suspense, as each survivor slowly but surely turns on his colleagues.

Crazy as it sounds, *The Thing* is not even Carpenter's greatest cinematic achievement (keep reading!), but its combination of natural storytelling and remarkable pre-CGI special effects demonstrates that this is a director at the very top of his game. Some even call it the high-water mark in Russell's acting career.

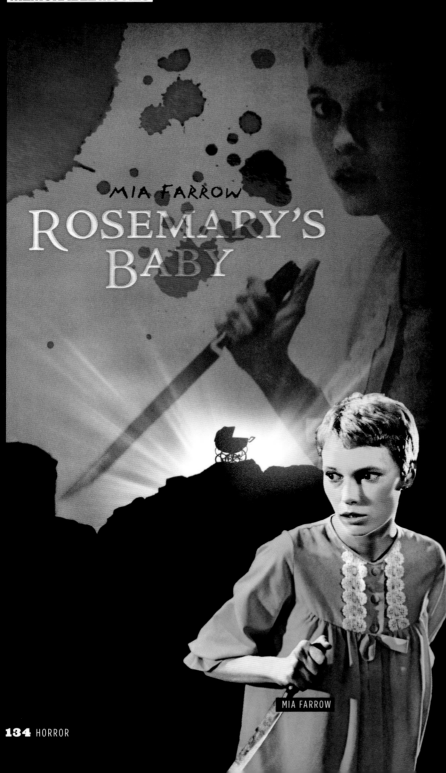

MIA FARROW

ROSEMARY'S BABY

MIA FARROW

7.
ROSEMARY'S BABY

1968 Roman Polanski's first Hollywood studio film lays on the tension from the very beginning, as young housewife Rosemary tries to get pregnant with her husband, struggling actor Guy. Soon, Guy befriends the odd next-door neighbors, and after Rosemary has a particularly troubling dream (in which she is ravaged by a beast), she does indeed become pregnant. That's when this film turns into a master class in horror.

Mia Farrow gives one of her best performances as Rosemary who, as she starts to realize that her husband might not be the father of her unborn child, also fears she is losing her mind. Polanski slowly ratchets up the pressure—on both Rosemary and the audience—until it becomes almost unbearable. As the Satanist next door, Ruth Gordon combines kindliness with creepiness so believably that she won an Academy Award for Best Supporting Actress. Mix it all together with an expectant parent's sense of dread and helplessness, and the result is terrifying. There's no blood, no gore and almost no violence, yet it is one of the most uncomfortable and disconcerting movies ever.

6.
POLTERGEIST

1982 At the heart of this evil ghost story lies a question: Who directed it? While Tobe Hooper is solely credited, many call it a Steven Spielberg film, as he conceived the story, co-wrote the screenplay and was reportedly on the set making most, if not all, of the key filmmaking decisions. But he had also directed *E.T. the Extra-Terrestrial*, which had hit theaters on June 11, 1982, a single week after *Poltergeist*. His *E.T.* contract said he couldn't direct another movie while working on that one. People involved with *Poltergeist* said he oversaw casting, directed the actors and designed every shot, but still, Hooper gets the credit.

It's a remarkable piece of work, about a normal family living in a house haunted by evil ghosts who kidnap the youngest daughter (Heather O'Rourke) and take her to a different dimension while terrorizing her parents and siblings. Playing off the fears of both children and adults—and anyone's issues with clowns and dolls, among other things— it's a pretty horrifying flick, whoever directed it.

ZELDA RUBINSTEIN

HEATHER O'ROURKE

OLIVER ROBINS

ELSA LANCHESTER

...more fearful than the monster himself!

CARL LAEMMLE
presents

The
BRIDE
OF
FRANKENSTEIN
starring KARLOFF

COLIN CLIVE   VALERIE HOBSON   ELSA LANCHESTER
ERNEST THESIGER   AND   E.E. CLIVE

PRODUCED BY CARL LAEMMLE JR.
SCREENPLAY BY WILLIAM HURLBUT & JOHN BALDERSTON

Directed by JAMES WHALE
A UNIVERSAL PICTURE

BORIS KARLOFF

5.
THE BRIDE OF FRANKENSTEIN

1935 The only sequel on this list is both the apex of the 1930s Universal Pictures monster craze and the best film that director James Whale ever made. Picking up pretty much where the first movie left off, it finds Dr. Frankenstein continuing to reanimate the dead, now creating a mate for his forlorn Creature. When the "bride" comes to life, she takes one look at the Creature and makes it clear that he is not her cup of tea, adding a heaping spoonful of tragedy onto the horror.

Critics call it a rehash of the first movie, and to some extent it is, but it takes many of that film's moments and builds on them, adding texture and emotion. While *Bride* contains many indelible images, perhaps the best is actress Elsa Lanchester's bloodcurdling scream upon first seeing her intended mate. Nothing from the first film has that impact. Deep pathos informs some of the best horror. It's hard to argue, even 80-plus years later, that the combination has been put to better use, before or since.

4.
JAWS

1975 When a movie actually makes you afraid to go into the water, you know it's doing its job. (Especially when that body of water is a backyard pool miles from any ocean. Sounds silly, but more than 40 years ago, it was a thing.) Steven Spielberg's first big studio movie almost went off the rails many times: The combination of an ocean shoot and the mechanical shark's malfunctions sent the film over budget and behind schedule. Amazingly, lack of a working shark only helped the finished product, as it allowed Spielberg to exploit the audience's fear by forcing viewers to imagine the terror rather than actually see it.

Jaws gets credit (or blame) for kicking off Hollywood's blockbuster era, but the movie is so much bigger than that. It addresses the primal fears of being in open water, of being prey for a larger animal and of nature having its way with you. It also lets the audience see the horror through the hero's eyes, as Roy Scheider's Chief Brody tries to save the townsfolk from a man-eating killer...and repeatedly fails. Add in the now iconic John Williams score, and never mind the horror genre—it's one of the greatest movies of any kind, ever.

SUSAN BACKLINIE

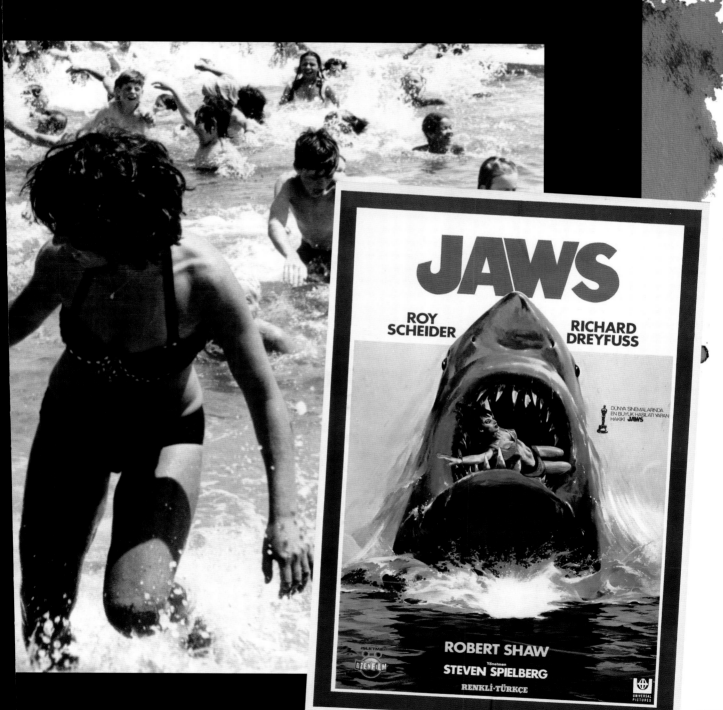

ALFRED HITCHCOCK'S
PSYCHO

JANET LEIGH

3.
PSYCHO

1960 Leave it to Alfred Hitchcock to create a whole new brand of horror: the slasher, which would become perhaps the most popular of all. And, while he was at it, he made a film so strong from start to finish, with so many different iconic moments, sequences and plot devices, that it remains one of the bright, shining examples of the genre. And 60 years later, that's still how we view *Psycho*. It's perhaps not as scary as it was, and some of the talk about mental illness is a bit dated, but the quality and impact remain.

The story of Norman Bates and his mother is the last truly great film that Hitch made, and it's a near-perfect example of proper story structure and how to build suspense. It would have to be, considering the number of times it's been examined, lampooned, copied, prequeled and sequeled and, in 1998, remade shot for shot. The shower scene alone might qualify it for this list—especially when you consider that star Janet Leigh never showered again, sticking forever after to baths—but that's just the most explosive and scary moment in a movie that explores the nature of duality. Ultimately, it's just a brilliant piece of cinema, no matter how you slice it.

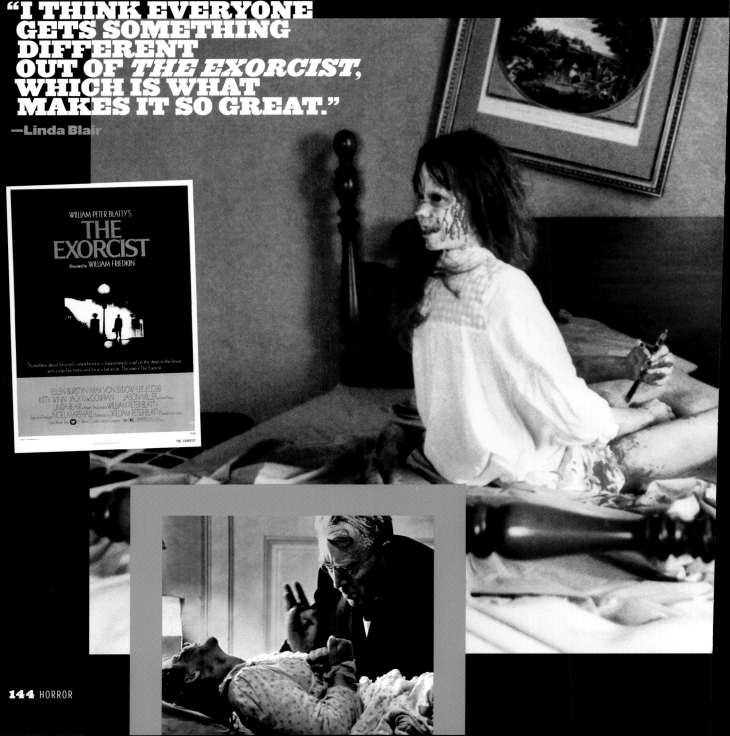

"I THINK EVERYONE GETS SOMETHING DIFFERENT OUT OF *THE EXORCIST*, WHICH IS WHAT MAKES IT SO GREAT."

—Linda Blair

2. THE EXORCIST

1973 Whether you believe in Satan or the concept of hell or demons or any of that stuff is immaterial when it comes to *The Exorcist*. The film is just really, really, *really* scary, regardless of your personal views or religion. William Peter Blatty adapted the script from his own best-selling novel—and won an Academy Award for it—and William Friedkin directed. Possessed by a demon, a young girl in the Georgetown neighborhood of Washington, D.C., must undergo an exorcism by two priests. Like *Rosemary's Baby*, the movie explores good versus evil and the perils and self-doubts of parenthood as well as the concept of faith. Unlike that film, it does so in a very visceral way.

The tragic story of young Regan MacNeil and Fathers Merrin and Karras is riveting from almost the very first moment, as viewers—like the characters on-screen—must question what they're seeing. *The Exorcist* culminates in an extended sequence in which the two priests are ready to sacrifice themselves to save the girl from a fate worse than death. The combination of symbolism, imagery and good old-fashioned scares makes this a classic.

TONY MORAN, AS
MICHAEL MYERS

HALLOWEEN

The
Night
He
Came
Home!

MUSTAPHA AKKAD PRESENTS DONALD PLEASENCE IN JOHN CARPENTER'S "HALLOWEEN"
WITH JAMIE LEE CURTIS, P.J. SOLES, NANCY LOOMIS. WRITTEN BY JOHN CARPENTER AND DEBRA HILL
EXECUTIVE PRODUCER IRWIN YABLANS. DIRECTED BY JOHN CARPENTER. PRODUCED BY DEBRA HILL
PANAVISION
© COMPASS INTERNATIONAL RELEASE

P. J. SOLES

1.
HALLOWEEN

1978 Was there really ever any doubt? It's hard to argue that any director has had a greater influence on the horror genre over the past 50 years than John Carpenter. You could make the case that *The Thing* is, from a purely technical perspective, a better film. Even so, the impact, influence, importance and timelessness of *Halloween* puts it at the very top of this list.

That, and the fact that it is just incredibly freaking scary—but that almost feels like the cherry on the sundae.

Carpenter's tale of child murderer Michael Myers, who grows up to be a maniac killing machine who hunts his teenage sister and her friends, starts out rough and then, after a brief period of normalcy, gets far rougher. It eventually builds to a crescendo of violence that would set the tone for several generations of horror films to follow. Just a few years into her acting career, Jamie Lee Curtis made her movie debut as Myers' sister, Laurie Strode (see page 118). The movie perfectly—and terrifyingly—shows how absolute evil can sprout from the mundane, and how a normal family can produce something as horrible as this masked killer.

Simply put, the film is a classic, from start to finish.

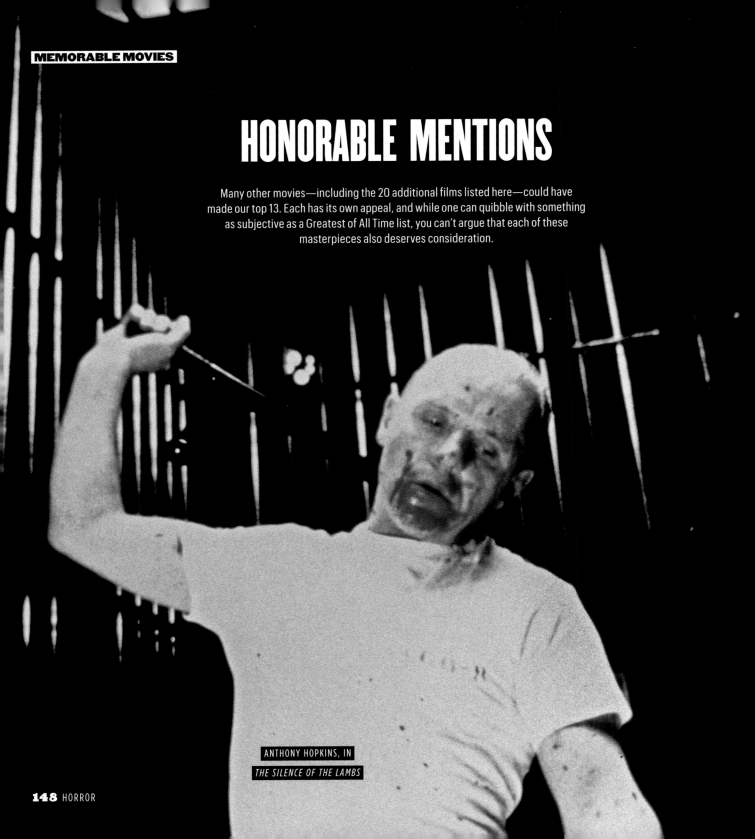

HONORABLE MENTIONS

Many other movies—including the 20 additional films listed here—could have made our top 13. Each has its own appeal, and while one can quibble with something as subjective as a Greatest of All Time list, you can't argue that each of these masterpieces also deserves consideration.

ANTHONY HOPKINS, IN
THE SILENCE OF THE LAMBS

28 DAYS LATER

THE CABIN IN THE WOODS

CARRIE

THE CONJURING

DRACULA

THE EVIL DEAD 2

THE FLY

FRANKENSTEIN

GET OUT

IT

LET THE RIGHT ONE IN

A NIGHTMARE ON ELM STREET

NOSFERATU

THE OMEN

THE RING

SAW

SHAUN OF THE DEAD

THE SHINING

THE SILENCE OF THE LAMBS

SUSPIRIA

149

SCREAM
WITH LAUGHTER

HACKING THROUGH A CENTURY OF HORROR PARODIES, FROM SILENT FILMS TO MOCKUMENTARIES.

Spoofs have been poking fun at horror for a century. Silent-film icon Harold Lloyd released *Haunted Spooks* in 1920, two years before F. W. Murnau's groundbreaking vampire film, *Nosferatu*. Throughout—and beyond—the '20s, silly horror-tinged comedies like *The Ghost Breaker*, *Dr. Pyckle and Mr. Pride* and *The Cat and the Canary* kept audiences laughing…nervously.

In the 1930s, thanks to Universal's monster series, true horror took center stage. One of those films, James Whale's *The Invisible Man* (adapted in 1933 from the H. G. Wells novel), is considered a parody, because it mocks the genre with its own tropes, or storytelling devices. The title character first discovers invisibility, then lets it corrupt him to the point of pure evil. In the end, invisibility betrays him. This smart,

well-made film is the second-best thing Whale ever directed, after *The Bride of Frankenstein* (1935).

More parodies followed, even into the '40s, but horror humor didn't go mainstream until the comedy duo of Bud Abbott and Lou Costello began making movies with monsters. In 1941, they made *Hold That Ghost*, then scored big in 1948 with *Abbott and Costello Meet Frankenstein*. At the time, the actors—especially Lou Costello— had their doubts. Costello ranted that his 5-year-old daughter could have written a funnier script, although he reportedly later warmed to the movie. The film was eventually lauded as a Hollywood classic, selected for preservation in the National Film Registry by the Library of Congress.

Universal soon milked the "meet" formula, pairing the duo with "the Killer, Boris Karloff" in

Tim Curry called
the *Rocky Horror*
midnight movie
mania "a guaranteed
weekend party...and
a chance for people to
try a few roles
on for size."

1949 (more crime than horror), then with the Invisible Man in 1951, and with Dr. Jekyll and Mr. Hyde in 1953 before the series died out with the Mummy in 1955.

In 1960, producer Roger Corman struck gold with *The Little Shop of Horrors*, a spoof about a man-eating plant and its human servant who must search out hapless victims. It became a cult sensation, eventually inspiring a live 1982 musical comedy production (still

performed in theaters today) and a 1986 movie based on that musical.

The 1960s saw such features as Corman's *Creature From the Haunted Sea*, *The Comedy of Terrors* (a slasher parody starring Vincent Price, Boris Karloff and Peter Lorre) and the Don Knotts vehicle *The Ghost and Mr. Chicken*.

In September 1964, TV became horror-parody central, when both *The Addams Family* and *The Munsters* premiered in the same

week. Though very different in tone, both shows played horror elements for laughs. As Herman Munster, Fred Gwynne looked like Frankenstein's creature, while both Yvonne De Carlo as Lily Munster and Carolyn Jones as Morticia Addams wore the vampire look well. The shows helped spark a horror-comedy boom, which really took off in the 1970s.

Meanwhile, in 1969, an animated Great Dane and his

Riding high off his Barney Fife fame from *The Andy Griffith Show*, Don Knotts starred with Joan Staley in the 1966 horror comedy *The Ghost and Mr. Chicken*.

CLAUDE RAINS, IN *THE INVISIBLE MAN*
1933

AUDREY II, IN *LITTLE SHOP OF HORRORS*
1986

LON CHANEY JR. AND LOU COSTELLO, IN *ABBOTT AND COSTELLO MEET FRANKENSTEIN*
1948

SCOOBY-DOO, WHERE ARE YOU!
1969

HAROLD LLOYD AND FRIEND, IN *HAUNTED SPOOKS*
1920

TOR JOHNSON (STANDING) AND MONA MCKINNON, IN *PLAN 9 FROM OUTER SPACE*
1959

The Original MONSTER MASH

four human friends began solving horror-themed crimes on the Saturday-morning cartoon series *Scooby-Doo, Where Are You!* This unlikely concept has yielded several TV series and feature films to date.

Among the Me Decade's many horror parodies, the most successful was Mel Brooks' *Young Frankenstein* (1974), which skewered the original story lovingly and mercilessly. Shot entirely in black and white, it even used the same lab equipment props employed in 1931's *Frankenstein*. Gene Wilder played the doctor, and Peter Boyle was his creature. Brooks himself adapted the movie into a Broadway musical in 2007.

The '70s also gave us *Attack of the Killer Tomatoes*, *Piranha* and the 1979 Dracula spoof *Love at First Bite*. But one of the biggest horror spoofs ever is *The Rocky Horror Picture Show*, starring Tim Curry, Susan Sarandon and Barry Bostwick. A colossal failure upon its 1975 release, this eccentric musical went on to become an influential and beloved cult film, inspiring countless midnight screenings and, some say, much of punk fashion (ripped fishnet stockings, androgyny, over-the-top makeup, etc.). And nearly 45 years after its premiere, the movie is still in limited release—making it the longest-running theatrical release in film. Devoted fans *still* show up for midnight screenings, where they pay tribute with props, shout out favorite lines and sing along.

Of course, as slasher films ran amok in the late 1970s and '80s, so did films that combined comedy with horror. Dozens of movies followed, ranging from B-listers like *Return of the Killer Tomatoes* to critical darlings like *An American Werewolf in London*.

Sam Raimi's 1987 sequel, *Evil Dead 2: Dead by Dawn*, is part parody, because it so knowingly plays the genre for screams and laughs. Meta horror comedy grew in the 1990s, reaching an

apex in 1996 with *Scream*. Wes Craven's masterful satire changed the game entirely (see sidebar, page 155). Without *Scream*, many great horror films of the past two decades wouldn't exist. There is the *Scary Movie* franchise, of course, which spoofs *Scream* itself, as well as many others, like *Cabin Fever*, *Tucker & Dale vs. Evil* and *Vampire Academy*—and we're not even including the second-best horror satire of all time, 2004's *Shaun of the Dead*.

In 2014, Jemaine Clement (of *Flight of the Conchords*) and

Taika Waititi made a very modern parody when they starred in, wrote and directed *What We Do in the Shadows*, a reality TV–style mockumentary about four nerdy vampires sharing a house in a New Zealand suburb.

Literary horror satire has had some high points. In 1890, Oscar Wilde wrote his ludicrous tale of horror, *The Picture of Dorian Gray*, a classic story of eternal youth. While literary horror parody popped up occasionally in the 20th century (mostly in comic books and collections like *Weird*

GEORGE HAMILTON AND SUSAN SAINT JAMES, IN *LOVE AT FIRST BITE* 1979

SCARY MOVIE 2000

Tales), it has flourished recently, encouraged by Seth Grahame-Smith's success. His first two books, *Pride and Prejudice and Zombies* (2009) and *Abraham Lincoln: Vampire Hunter* (2010), were both best sellers, even if the movie adaptations disappointed. In general, books that traffic in supernatural humor are more popular than ever these days.

While horror has waxed and waned over the years, we're at peak horror now. And when a genre does well, parody is sure to follow. ▬

Horror master Wes Craven on the set of *Nightmare on Elm Street*.

WES CRAVEN POKES FUN AT HIS OWN LEGACY

Believe it or not, Wes Craven originally declined to direct *Scream*, the movie that would define him as much as *The Last House on the Left* and the *Nightmare on Elm Street* series did. While those are both significant landmarks of film history, *Scream* changed the way audiences look at and understand horror. It showed how the genre operates while scaring us out of our wits.

Yet the humor in the script (originally titled *Scary Movie*) is what initially turned Craven off. Only later, after rereading it several times, did he finally get the vision and ask to direct it. With Craven at the helm, fans saw that the movie took the genre seriously even as it poked fun. As Dimension Films head Bob Weinstein wrote after Craven's 2015 death, "In 1996, the genre almost died out. Wes Craven brought the genre back, with the start of the *Scream* franchise. It is considered a seminal film in the anthology of horror movies, and the overwhelming credit goes to the master, Wes Craven."

DARK SHADOWS, 1966

TV & BOOKS

AMERICAN HORROR STORY: HOTEL, 2015

SMALL SCREEN, BIG SCARES

HOW TV EVOLVED, FROM *THE TWILIGHT ZONE* TO *THE X-FILES* TO TODAY'S EXPLOSION OF AWESOME WEEKLY HORROR SHOWS.

Horror was a popular movie genre almost from the birth of moving pictures, but it took TV a while to catch on. Soap operas and comedies ruled in the early days, but it wasn't until the great Rod Serling turned his attention to the small screen that an era began.

Serling's masterwork is called *The Twilight Zone*. While it focused primarily on unsettling tales of sci-fi, fantasy and the supernatural, it sometimes veered into outright horror (see sidebar, page 164). After its 1959 debut, the doors swung open, and other series soon followed. First and foremost was *The Outer Limits*. Debuting in 1963, it skewed more toward science fiction, but went darker than *The Twilight Zone*. The show lasted for only two seasons and 49 episodes, but was revived from 1995 to 2002.

In 1966, ABC premiered the soap opera *Dark Shadows*, which showcased vampire Barnabas Collins and his clan in the fictional town of Collinsport, Maine. Beyond vampires, there were also werewolves, ghosts, monsters, witches, warlocks and plenty of other craziness that made the soap a big hit throughout a five-year, 1,200-plus-episode run.

In 1969, Serling returned to the airwaves with *Night Gallery*, which was more horror-focused than *The Twilight Zone* had been. Like that series and *The Outer Limits*, *Gallery* was an anthology show. It presented three unconnected single-episode stories each week. It has its fans, but the show gets less love than Serling's earlier series. It may be known best for featuring Steven Spielberg's professional directorial debut in 1969.

DAVID McCALLUM,
IN *THE OUTER LIMITS*
1963

In January 1972, *The Night Stalker* brought television viewers some serious gore and hard-core scares. The made-for-TV movie starred Darren McGavin as investigative reporter Carl Kolchak, who comes to believe a vampire is behind a series of grisly deaths in Las Vegas. Its popularity led to a sequel in 1973, *The Night Strangler*, and then a series in 1974. *Kolchak: The Night Stalker* only lasted one season, but it is widely recognized as a major

inspiration for *The X-Files*, which premiered 18 years after *Kolchak* went off the air.

In between, of course, there were other shows, like George Romero's *Tales from the Dark Side*, *Friday the 13th: The Series* and *Tales from the Crypt*. Each had some success, but none measure up to the depth and quality of *The X-Files*. Created by Chris Carter, the show straddled the line between science fiction and horror, often bouncing back

and forth between them. It made stars of David Duchovny and Gillian Anderson, and many of its writers—Vince Gilligan (*Breaking Bad*, *Better Call Saul*), Howard Gordon (*24*, *Homeland*), Kim Manners (*Supernatural*) and Frank Spotnitz (*The Man in the High Castle*)—went on to create major new series. On top of that, the list of shows *The X-Files* has influenced or inspired could be a chapter all its own: *Strange World*, *The Burning Zone*, *Lost*,

MISHA COLLINS, IN *SUPERNATURAL* 2019

DARREN McGAVIN, IN *KOLCHAK: THE NIGHT STALKER* 1974

SARAH MICHELLE GELLAR, IN *BUFFY THE VAMPIRE SLAYER* 1998

DAVID DUCHOVNY AND GILLIAN ANDERSON, IN *THE X-FILES* 1997

JONATHAN IN *DARK SH* 1966

HORROR

DARK MISTRESS

Of all the late-night horror hosts in all the towns, one stands tall: Cassandra Peterson's Elvira and her *Movie Macabre* show. A former Vegas showgirl who lost her virginity to Tom Jones, appeared in a Bond movie and dated Elvis Presley, she got the job after the death of *Fright Night* host Sinister Seymour (aka Larry Vincent). Inspired by Vampira, the darkly comic '50s "glamour ghoul" created by actress Maila Nurmi, the show's producers wanted another horror hostess. (Vampira was in turn inspired by the creepy, slinky matriarch in Charles Addams' cartoons—later known as Morticia on TV's *The Addams Family*.) Peterson was performing at LA's Groundlings improv theater when the producers saw her and cast her. She combined valley-girl lingo, humor and over-the-top sex appeal to become a household name and hosted her syndicated show for seven years. She also made three movies (including 1988's classic *Elvira, Mistress of the Dark*) and still plays the role, off and on, to this day.

The Walking Dead star Andrew Lincoln finally left the show in 2018 after more than eight seasons.

Dark Skies, *The Visitor Fringe* and *Warehouse 13* are all direct descendants. Joss Whedon described his beloved series *Buffy the Vampire Slayer* (1997–2003) as *The X-Files* meets *My So-Called Life*. That right there is some serious influence.

Speaking of *Buffy*, Whedon's series was itself a major achievement, a unique blend of horror, comedy, camp, contemplation and teen angst. It, too, was unlike anything that had come before it (apart from the 1992 movie that inspired it), which is why it fits so well here. Indeed, so much of the horror that has appeared on television has been groundbreaking in some way, giving viewers something new, thought-provoking and, obviously, scary.

That helps explain why we're in the midst of a Golden Age of horror TV. There's not just a lot of horror on the small screen—there's a widely diverse range of shows.

American Horror Story is an anthology that bounces back and forth in time and location, heaping on the creep factor, thanks to creator Ryan Murphy's wild vision. *The Walking Dead* and its prequel spinoff, *Fear the Walking Dead*, are set in a world where a zombie-creating virus has ended society as we know it, forcing the survivors to navigate a harsh and scary new reality. *Scream* is based on the hit movie series. The 2020 series *Locke & Key* blends fantasy and horror, while *Supernatural* has drawn viewers since 2005 with its story of two brothers who hunt monsters, demons and other otherworldly beings. Meanwhile, *Stranger Things*, inspired by many great '80s films, has become a generation-spanning sensation all its own; parents love the nostalgia, kids love the kid stars and everyone loves how creepy and bingeable it is. It's an impressive list, especially considering that these shows are mostly all running at the same time.

Recent fare also included a number of other entertaining options. *iZombie*—a lighthearted take on the genre—was adapted from a comic book that was more fun than frightening. *Outcast*, a dark series from *Walking Dead* creator Robert Kirkman, dealt in demonic possession. *The Vampire Diaries* spinoff *The Originals* followed a family of vampires. We also had *Preacher*, *The Strain*, *Bates Motel*, *Teen Wolf*, *Grimm*, *Hannibal*, *Fringe* and yes, a briefly revived *The X-Files* to choose from. Stay tuned: More horror shows are coming up—after this brief word from our sponsors. ◼

163

The Twilight Zone
DAWN OF A GENRE

hanks to syndication, even very young ans have heard Rod Serling intone, "It is a dimension as vast as space and as timeless s infinity. It is the middle ground between ight and shadow, between science and uperstition, and it lies between the pit of nan's fears and the summit of his knowledge. his is the dimension of imagination. It is n area which we call the Twilight Zone." he groundbreaking show began with these vords, giving the audience fair warning.

For five seasons, starting in 1959, Serling nd his team on *The Twilight Zone* told eerie tories that often ended with a twist. Like the episode about a bookworm who just wants to be alone so he can read. An apocalypse leaves nim, the sole survivor, happily stranded with a lifetime supply of books. Then...he breaks his glasses. Or the episode "To Serve Man," in which aliens bring a book thought to be about helping humanity. The episode title is also the book's title, and it's actually... a cookbook!

The show commented on society by spotlighting shared fears—and using our own anxieties to entertain us. Most episodes also offered some soft-sell moralizing that kept viewers thinking long after the credits had rolled. Two revivals and one feature film have tried to re-create Serling's vision; a third reboot, shepherded and narrated by Oscar-winning *Get Out* writer-director Jordan Peele, premiered on the CBS All Access streaming service in 2019.

ROD SERLING,
IN *THE TWILIGHT ZONE*
1963

RICHARD KIEL,
IN *THE TWILIGHT ZONE*
1962

The Twilight Zone blended mystery, suspense and social commentary.

WILLIAM D. GORDON AND
JENNIFER HOWARD,
IN *THE TWILIGHT ZONE*
1960

BOOKS OF THE
DEAD

HOW LITERARY HORROR ROSE FROM ANCIENT CAMPFIRES TO PULP FICTION TO MAINSTREAM RESPECTABILITY.

The written word requires readers to scare themselves, using the power of imagination. Some would say that things you can't see are scarier than what's right in front of you, but painting a truly terrifying picture with words isn't easy. That's why authors who specialize in horror have such rabid followings: Readers know they'll be scared out of their wits by whatever they find between the covers.

Sitting around a campfire telling ghost stories wasn't invented at modern summer camps. The literary horror tradition goes back millennia, and people have been telling scary stories for longer than we can speculate. Told and retold through the ages, some legends eventually became poems, long-form sagas and scary fairy tales.

The earliest literary reference to a werewolf showed up in a poem from ancient Mesopotamia called the "Epic of Gilgamesh," written around 2100 B.C. Sometime in the Dark Ages, between 700 and 1000 A.D., someone (or something) wrote the story of Beowulf, a brave warrior who fights a monster called Grendel. In 1812, two German brothers, Jacob and Wilhelm Grimm, collected 86 fairy tales— some of them quite terrifying—into a book. It was so popular that by 1857, the seventh edition had grown to contain 211 tales.

But it was a fateful night on the shore of Lake Geneva that really launched our modern literary horror tradition. Yes, that was the night Mary Shelley dreamed up the demented doctor and pathetic creature she would immortalize in 1818's *Frankenstein: Or, the Modern Prometheus* (see page 28). That same night, Lord Byron invented—and discarded—an idea

EDGAR ALLAN POE

GRENDEL TOYS WITH
BEOWULF, AS DRAWN BY
HECTOR CASANOVA

about a vampire. It inspired his own doctor, John Polidori, to write *The Vampyre*. First published in 1819 in a magazine—78 years before Bram Stoker's *Dracula*—the story was soon translated into five languages. It inspired plays in English and French, and even an opera in German.

The name of Edgar Allan Poe (1809–1849) is synonymous with the beginnings of literary horror. We're still reading and shivering at the gothic drama of poems like "The Raven" and stories like "The Black Cat" and "The Pit and the Pendulum." Poe died almost 50 years before Stoker published his seminal work.

In 1847, the year Stoker was born, Thomas Preskett Prest's wildly popular 228-chapter serial, *Varney the Vampire*, was published in novel form. In 1872, Sheridan Le Fanu published *Carmilla* (see page 14). The first book about a female vampire, it is second only to *Dracula* as a literary source for vampire films.

So by 1897, the reading public was primed for Stoker's novel *Dracula*. The book combined the setting and myths of central Europe with John Polidori's suave Anglophile demon and *Carmilla*'s sensual, atmospheric language. Jack the Ripper, a real-life English serial killer of the late 1880s, may have been another inspiration. And the rest, as they say, is history.

As gripping as horror was in the late 1800s, it really came into its own in the 20th century. As times changed, so did the scares. Authors were ready to take audiences to new levels of imagination and terror—and readers were ready for the ride. Stoker's staid, Victorian writing gave way to the much more vivid work of H. P. Lovecraft. Though he died broke in 1937 at age 46, he's now widely recognized as one of horror's best and most influential authors.

Lovecraft's work, often involving a cosmic entity known as Cthulhu, explored deep issues that challenged readers in new ways. He delved into themes of forbidden knowledge, nonhuman influences and the ability of so-called "savages" to understand things that "civilized" people could not, as well as traditional ideas like guilt and fate. Years after his death, Lovecraft's name became synonymous with horror in a way he probably never imagined. He is also credited as being an early practitioner of science fiction.

In his wake came authors like Richard Matheson, Shirley Jackson, Ray Bradbury and Ira Levin, who explored dark and gothic themes in modern contexts. Their advances helped pave the way for the man who is, without question, the genre's defining author of the past 50 years—perhaps even of all time.

BRAM STOKER

MARY SHELLEY

H. P. LOVECRAFT

SHIRLEY JACKSON

STEPHEN KING

"MONSTERS ARE REAL, AND GHOSTS ARE REAL TOO. THEY LIVE INSIDE US, AND SOMETIMES THEY WIN."

—Stephen King

Stephen King first came to prominence in 1973 with *Carrie*, though he'd been selling stories for several years. That hit novel launched a string of best sellers that would continue almost unbroken to this day. There is no type or style of horror that King won't take on, including vampires (*Salem's Lot*), werewolves (*Silver Bullet*), ghosts (*The Shining*), the end of the world (*The Stand*), rabid animals (*Cujo*), demonic possession (*Christine*), witches and warlocks (*Thinner*), a supernatural killer clown (*It*), evil technology (*Cell*), gothic (*Misery*), zombies (*Pet Sematary*), and the Devil (*Needful Things*). Pure, unadulterated evil is his specialty. He's branched out past horror, but his best-known works are in that genre. Over the years, King has become one of the most respected writers in the English language, which has in turn brought greater legitimacy to the genre.

While King paved the way for horror's literary boom, some of his contemporaries were also integral to that success. Dean Koontz is one of King's favorites and has written dozens of best sellers himself, including modern classics like *Watchers* and *Phantoms*, to name just two. Peter Straub is another. In addition to co-writing the *Talisman* trilogy of novels with King, Straub has been churning out popular horror fiction for more than four decades. Clive Barker not only writes best-selling horror novels, he's also a respected film director who has adapted his own works for the big screen—first *Hellraiser* (1987) and then *Nightbreed* and *Lord of Illusions*, both in the '90s.

And this isn't just a man's game. Anne Rice (see page 23) has sold millions of books about vampires, witches and other things that go bump in the night. Then there's Joyce Carol Oates; accomplished in a variety of types of fiction and criticism, her horror work—including *American Gothic Tales*, *The Accursed* and *Zombie*—is impressive. These authors and others have elevated and expanded

ANNE RICE

the field, moving it from the realm of pulp fiction and fan magazines into the mainstream. This evolution has paved a path for such younger authors as Jonathan Maberry, Mylo Carbia, Justin Cronin, Michael Anderle, Shayne Silvers, Raye Wagner and King's own sons, Joe Hill and Owen King.

Horror movies are big again, and so are horror books. So keep turning those pages…if you dare! ➡

see page 23

HEAR THE HORROR

As much as we love scary movies and TV, audio horror taps into the most powerful source of terror: the imagination. Its frights and delights go way back, from campfire ghost stories to pre-TV radio shows that united the whole family.

Today, podcasts make it easy to enjoy horror anywhere you go—whether it's on a walk, in the car or deep, deep under the covers. They come in three main categories: fiction, nonfiction and fanzine-like discussions of horror movies and TV.

Fiction is most popular horror podcast format, spanning a spectrum of formats and styles. Some rely on classic tropes, like vampires and ghosts, while others mine the terrors of modern life. Many mix up a witches' brew of classic horror, supernatural weirdness, urban legends and true crime. *The Horror!* re-airs old-time radio shows with context and backstory. *Pseudopod* and *The Other Stories*, for example, feature highly produced short stories—a successful approach also heard on *The No Sleep Podcast*, which grew out of a popular subreddit full of user-generated stories and "creepypastas" (horror written for the web).

Top serials include *Welcome to Night Vale* (the eerie, ever-expanding world of a fictional town) and the newer *Cryptids* (sci-fi, conspiracy theories and imaginary creatures). Some riff on NPR-style investigative podcasts like the megahit *Serial*. *The Black Tapes* dramatizes supernatural stories as does *Limetown*, which spawned a video series on Facebook Watch.

In the nonfiction area, top-rated *Lore* spawned an Amazon Prime TV series. WNYC's *Spooked* features "true" supernatural stories told by people who survived them. *True Crime Horror Story* is exactly what it sounds like.

You can hear fans talk about horror movies on *Last Podcast on the Left* and *The Nightmare on Film Street*, but to hear top creators talk, check out *Shock Waves*, a co-production of horror heroes Blumhouse and Fangoria.

A QUIET PLACE, 2018

MODERN FRIGHTS

SMARTER, SCARIER, FREAKIER, RICHER: SURVEYING THE BLISTERED, FERTILE LANDSCAPE OF CONTEMPORARY HORROR.

This is a golden age of horror. Not just on the big screen but on TV, in books, in video games, on podcasts and probably in community theater and with finger puppets. There's simply no denying it—we love our scares. And nowhere has that translated to greater innovation and enrichment than in movies.

Following a late-20th-century slump, the genre has been on a roll. Just about every subgenre draws audiences, especially when it comes to low-budget films that occasionally explode into the zeitgeist. Filmmakers who got their start making small movies end up directing films with nine-figure budgets. James Wan went from the no-budget *Saw* in 2004 to *Furious 7* in 2015 and *Aquaman* in 2018. Neil Marshall made his bones on *The Descent* in 2005, and in 2019 he oversaw the studio reboot of *Hellboy*.

Both of those early films typify how horror is made and viewed today. *Saw* didn't usher in the torture-porn era, but it did solidify the subgenre, wherein victims are dispatched in increasingly grisly and imaginative ways. Similarly, *The Descent* took the idea of a female-led horror film—hardly a new idea—to the next level, with an *entirely* female cast. It begins innocently enough, with a bunch of friends exploring a cave—until they stumble upon creatures that pick them off, one by one.

It's terrifying—and in the years since, more female-led horror flicks have been front and center, certainly in terms of actors, but also behind the camera. For example, Jennifer Kent wrote and directed *Monster* (2004) and *The Babadook* (2014). Diablo Cody wrote and Karyn Kusama directed *Jennifer's Body* (2009),

SHAWNEE SMITH,
IN *SAW*
2004

The *Saw* franchise
helped introduce
"torture porn" horror—
and made the careers of
writer-directors James
Wan (*Aquaman*) and
Leigh Whannell
(*The Invisible Man*).

175

NOAH WISEMAN AND ESSIE DAVIS,
IN *THE BABADOOK*
2014

DIRECTOR JAMES WAN

KRISTEN CONNOLLY,
IN *CABIN IN THE WOODS*
2011

Ana Lily Amirpour directed *A Girl Walks Home Alone at Night* (2014)—and so on.

Horror's not just getting better about gender; it's also getting better at making people think, as seen in movies like *The Babadook*, *The Cabin in the Woods*, *Split*, *You're Next*, *Unfriended*, *Attack the Block*, *Sinister*, *The Conjuring*, *Insidious*, *It Follows*, *The Purge*, *Happy Death Day* and *The Witch*, to name a few. While plenty of lowbrow genre pictures are hitting theaters, higher-end horror tends to give audiences more credit. A generation of fans was raised on movies like *Scream* and *The Sixth Sense*, which expect viewers to keep up, without any dumbing-down or overexplaining.

Not every horror film is like that, of course, but the trend is toward new and more interesting ways to scare people. Just check out Jordan Peele's 2017 flick *Get Out*, which won an Oscar for Best Original Screenplay. Rarely has a movie so electrified pop culture with a topical theme so well, uh, executed. Serious, funny and terrifying all at once, this so-called "social horror" film spawned hundreds of opinion pieces about film's place in society and its power of commentary. It also pulled in $176 million worldwide.

Consider, too, *Don't Breathe*, a 2016 hit that turned the

JANE LEVY, IN *DON'T BREATHE* 2016

JESSICA ROTHE, IN *HAPPY DEATH DAY* 2017

THE PURGE 2013

SHAUNA MACDONALD, IN *THE DESCENT* 2005

177

concept of a burglary gone wrong completely on its head. The third-act reveal was controversial (no spoilers here!), but the film made more than $150 million worldwide, working with a budget of less than $10 million. Sure, audiences like to be scared, but more and more, they also like to be treated with a modicum of respect while it's happening.

That's why movies like *It*, *Get Out* and *Split* did such enormous business in 2017. It's also why actor/filmmaker John Krasinski can not only make a huge hit like *A Quiet Place* but can cast an even bigger star, Emily Blunt (his wife), as the female lead. It's why M. Night Shyamalan can not only cast James McAvoy to play the lead in *Split* but also bring him back—and

BILL SKARSGÅRD, IN *IT*
2017

JORDAN PEELE, WITH HIS SCREENWRITING OSCAR FOR *GET OUT*

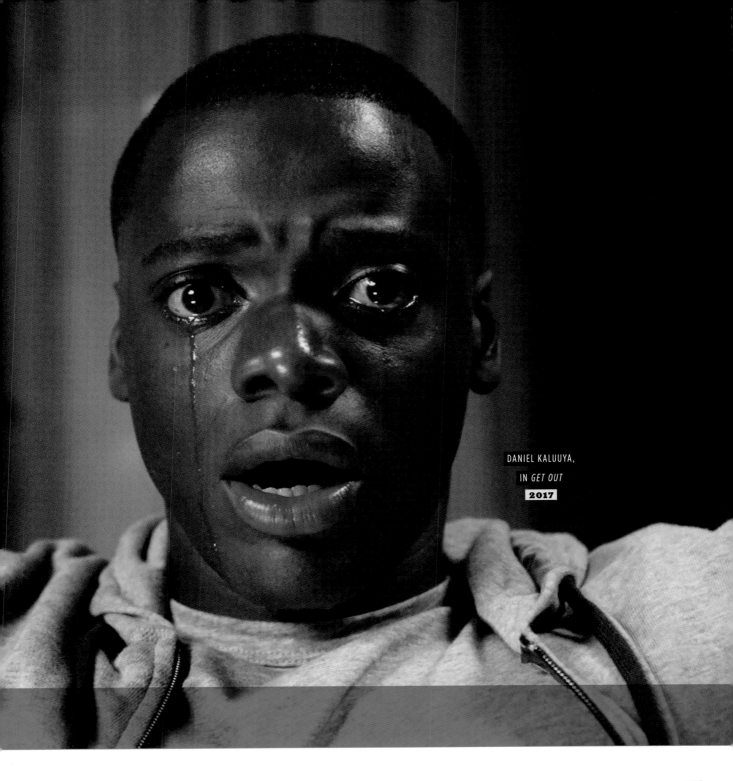

DANIEL KALUUYA,
IN *GET OUT*
2017

add Bruce Willis and Samuel L. Jackson—for the sequel, *Glass*, which premiered in 2019. It's why Jamie Lee Curtis returned to the *Halloween* franchise in 2018, this time with respected filmmakers David Gordon Green and Danny McBride behind the project.

Horror has new credibility, not only in Hollywood but also with growing audiences that keep lining up to have the wits scared out of them. And with numerous franchises and sequels coming over the next few years, there's no end in sight. ▬

JAMES McAVOY, IN *SPLIT*
2016

TERROR KNOWS NO BORDERS

So you think American horror is the best? That auteurs like Dario Argento, Guillermo del Toro, Takashi Miike, Kim Jee-woo and the filmmakers behind the late '90s/early '00s resurgence of Japanese horror (like Takashi Shimizu of *Ju-On: The Grudge* and Hideo Nakata of *Ringu*) just take their cues from American directors?

Poppycock. Great horror is global, and alien perspectives can be the creepiest. One of the most influential horror flicks ever is *Nosferatu*, the 1922 vampire movie from German director F. W. Murnau. In 1977, Argento helped define both the slasher and supernatural genres with his classic *Suspiria*. In 2018, Luca Guadagnino (*Call Me by Your Name*) remade the film with stars Dakota Johnson, Tilda Swinton and Mia Goth; Radiohead's Thom Yorke scored the film. Del Toro won Best Picture and Director Oscars for 2017's *The Shape of Water* (see page 58), but he's been making influential horror movies for decades, including *Cronos, The Devil's Backbone* and *Pan's Labyrinth*. He also co-wrote *The Strain* novels and co-created *The Strain* TV series. His credits include *Hellboy* (and its sequel), *Blade II, Mimic, Crimson Peak* and many others.

Such movies as Miike's *Audition* (Japan), *Thirst* (South Korea) and *Shutter* (Thailand) show that terror knows no borders. In fact, Japanese horror colonized the U.S. box office for a few years, driving big-name remakes like *The Ring* with Naomi Watts and *The Grudge* with noted Scream Queen Sarah Michelle Gellar.

Over the years, foreign horror's impact on the U.S. mainstream—from the Hammer movies out of England to Italian *giallo* slasher films to Spanish-language movies and more recent Asian films—has been clear and present...and growing.

YUYA OZEKI, IN
JU-ON: THE GRUDGE
2003

18

Attack the Block, 2011

A Quiet Place, 2018

Paranormal Activity, 2009

3:53:43 AM

The Babadook, 2014

The Purge, 2013

Saw, 2004

Us, 2019

Glass, 2019

BLUMHOUSE, THE LITTLE MOVIE STUDIO THAT COULD

How hard could it be? You make a horror movie with a commercial theme, cast a few recognizable faces, keep expenses low, release it into a few thousand theaters, then just count the cash. Sounds simple, right? Yet only producer Jason Blum's Blumhouse Pictures seems to know how to pull it off.

Paranormal Activity, *Insidious*, *Unfriended* and *The Purge*, which have all spawned their own franchises, are Blumhouse films. So are *Get Out*, *Happy Death Day* (a horror version of *Groundhog Day*) and the movies that revived M. Night Shyamalan's career: *The Visit* and *Split*. To top it all off, Blumhouse is also making *Halloween Kills*.

"When you do a movie for a low budget, the pressure to be a financial success goes down exponentially," Blum said in 2015. "Generally, the creative process is hurt if you're thinking about the end as opposed to focusing on day-to-day decisions and... taking chances; I really encourage the filmmakers we're working with to try new things and take advantage of the fact that we're working with a low budget so that they can take creative risks."

More often than not, those risks pay off. Some argue that the company makes many movies it never releases at all, focusing instead on those with greater chance of success. But it's hard to argue with that success, especially when it allows the company to make more mainstream projects, like the HBO series *Sharp Objects* (starring Amy Adams) and Spike Lee's *BlacKkKlansman*, both of which came out in 2018.

BLUMHOUSE CHIEF
JASON BLUM

TIME LINE

Meet Max Schreck, the vampire in F. W. Murnau's 1922 silent classic, *Nosferatu*.

VAMPIRES
NOSFERATU · DRACULA · MARK OF THE VAMPIRE · SON OF DRACULA · THE RETURN OF THE VAMPIRE · HOUSE OF DRACULA · DRACULA · THE CURSE OF DRACULA · VAMPIRA · SLAUGHTER OF THE VAMPIRE · THE KISS OF THE VAMPIRE · THE LAST MAN ON EARTH · DRACULA: PRINCE OF DARKNESS · A TASTE OF BLOOD · TASTE THE BLOOD OF DRACULA · BLACULA · DRACULA A.D. 1972 · NOSFERATU THE VAMPIRE · SALEM'S LOT

FRANKENSTEIN
FRANKENSTEIN · BRIDE OF FRANKENSTEIN · SON OF FRANKENSTEIN · THE HOUSE OF FRANKENSTEIN · THE GHOST OF FRANKENSTEIN · ABBOTT AND COSTELLO MEET FRANKENSTEIN · THE CURSE OF FRANKENSTEIN · THE REVENGE OF FRANKENSTEIN · FRANKENSTEIN 1970 · THE EVIL OF FRANKENSTEIN · FRANKENSTEIN CREATED WOMAN · THE HORROR OF FRANKENSTEIN · BLACKENSTEIN · FLESH FOR FRANKENSTEIN

WEREWOLVES
WEREWOLF OF LONDON · THE WOLF MAN · FRANKENSTEIN MEETS THE WOLF MAN · DAUGHTER OF THE WEREWOLF · SHE-WOLF OF LONDON · I WAS A TEENAGE WEREWOLF · THE CURSE OF THE WEREWOLF · FACE OF THE SCREAMING WEREWOLF · WEREWOLVES ON WHEELS · LEGEND OF THE WEREWOLF

MUMMIES
THE MUMMY · THE MUMMY'S HAND · THE MUMMY'S TOMB · THE MUMMY'S CURSE · THE MUMMY'S GHOST · THE MUMMY · PHARAOH'S CURSE · ATTACK OF THE MAYAN MUMMY · THE CURSE OF THE MUMMY'S TOMB · THE MUMMY'S SHROUD · BLOOD FROM THE MUMMY'S TOMB

MONSTERS, ETC.
THE PHANTOM OF THE OPERA · DR. JEKYLL AND MR. HYDE · FREAKS · KING KONG · THE FACE BEHIND THE MASK · DR. JEKYLL AND MR. HYDE · PHANTOM OF THE OPERA · CREATURE FROM THE BLACK LAGOON · GODZILLA · THE FLY · THE TINGLER · EYES WITHOUT A FACE · THE PHANTOM OF THE OPERA · IT · THE ABOMINABLE DR. PHIBES · JAWS · TRILOGY OF TERROR

ZOMBIES
WHITE ZOMBIE · REVOLT OF THE ZOMBIES · I WALKED WITH A ZOMBIE · REVENGE OF THE ZOMBIES · ISLE OF THE DEAD · THE PLAGUE OF THE ZOMBIES · I EAT YOUR SKIN · NIGHT OF THE LIVING DEAD · DAWN OF THE DEAD

Carol Ohmart and friend, in 1959's *House on Haunted Hill*

SLASHERS
THE PROWLER · PEEPING TOM · PSYCHO · STRAIT-JACKET · TWO THOUSAND MANIACS · REPULSION · THE HONEYMOON KILLERS · THE LAST HOUSE ON THE LEFT · THE TEXAS CHAIN SAW MASSACRE · SUSPIRIA · BLACK CHRISTMAS · THE HILLS HAVE EYES · I SPIT ON YOUR GRAVE · HALLOWEEN · PHANTASM

More than meets the eye: In 1933, Claude Rains was *The Invisible Man*.

SUPERNATURAL
THE OLD DARK HOUSE · THE BLACK CAT · THE RAVEN · CAT PEOPLE · THE PICTURE OF DORIAN GRAY · THE QUEEN OF SPADES · THE UNDEAD · I BURY THE LIVING · HOUSE ON HAUNTED HILL · DR. SARDONICUS · THE SHADOW OF THE CAT · THE HORRIBLE DR. HICHCOCK · CARNIVAL OF SOULS · BLACK SABBATH · THE INNOCENTS · THE HAUNTING · THE WICKER MAN · DON'T LOOK NOW · CARRIE · THE AMITYVILLE HORROR

DEMONS
KILL, BABY... KILL! · ROSEMARY'S BABY · THE EXORCIST · THE OMEN

SCI-FI
THE ISLAND OF LOST SOULS · THE INVISIBLE MAN · THE INVISIBLE MAN RETURNS · THE APE MAN · THE THING FROM ANOTHER WORLD · HOUSE OF WAX · INVADERS FROM MARS · THE QUATERMASS XPERIMENT · INVASION OF THE BODY SNATCHERS · THE BLOB · THEM! · THE CRAWLING EYE · ATTACK OF THE 50 FOOT WOMAN · VILLAGE OF THE DAMNED · THE DAY OF THE TRIFFIDS · THE BIRDS · THE LAST MAN ON EARTH · PLANET OF THE VAMPIRES · THE SORCERERS · INVASION OF THE BODY SNATCHERS · ALIEN · THE BROOD

PARODY
THE GHOST BREAKERS · SPOOKS RUN WILD · KING OF THE ZOMBIES · ZOMBIES ON BROADWAY · THE KILLER · ABBOTT AND COSTELLO MEET BORIS KARLOFF · I LIKE A VAMPIRE · THE LITTLE SHOP OF HORRORS · THE COMEDY OF TERRORS · MAD MONSTER PARTY? · MUNSTER, GO HOME · THE FEARLESS VAMPIRE KILLERS · THE MALTESE BIPPY · YOUNG FRANKENSTEIN · THE ROCKY HORROR PICTURE SHOW · LOVE AT FIRST BITE

↻ = Spawned one or more sequels

✳ This is a subjective selection of major movies judged by influence and/or income. It is by no means an exhaustive list. Your movies may vary.

1920 1930 1940 1950 1960 1970

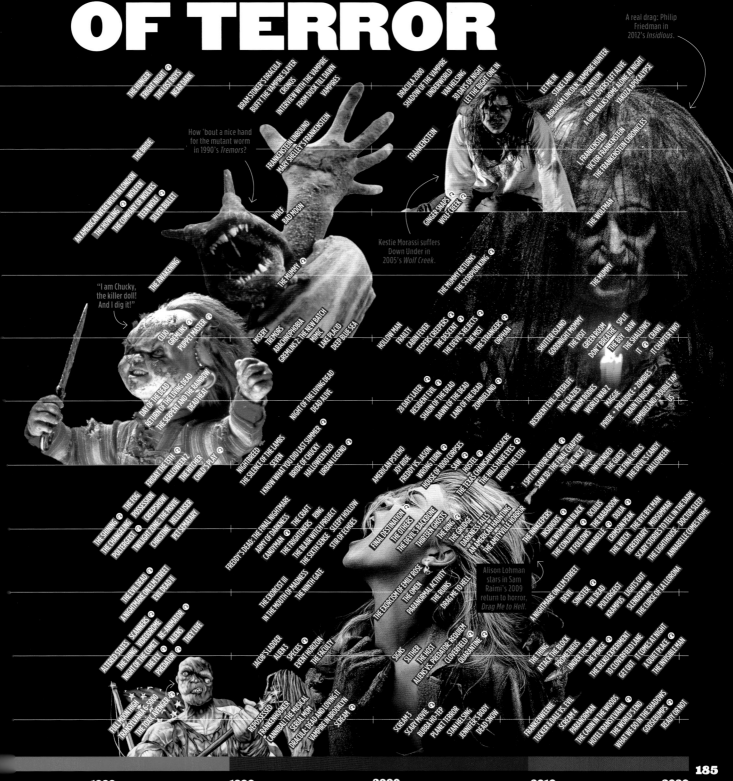

OF TERROR

A real drag: Philip Friedman in 2012's *Insidious*.

How 'bout a nice hand for the mutant worm in 1990's *Tremors*?

Kestie Morassi suffers Down Under in 2005's *Wolf Creek*.

"I am Chucky, the killer doll! And I dig it!"

Alison Lohman stars in Sam Raimi's 2009 return to horror, *Drag Me to Hell*.

1980 1990 2000 2010 2020

Cover Boonchuay Promjiam/Getty Images; shtiel/Shutterstock; United Archives GmbH/Alamy Stock Photo; ScreenProd/Photononstop/Alamy Stock Photo; DIMENSION FILMS/Album/Alamy Stock Photo; PhotoFest; AF archive/Alamy Stock Photo; PhotoFest; Pictorial Press Ltd/Alamy Stock Photo; Photo 12/Alamy Stock Photo; Courtesy of AMC; Moviestore Collection Ltd/Alamy Stock Photo; ScreenProd/Photononstop/Alamy Stock Photo; Brooke Palmer/Warner Bros. /Everett Collection; Johner Images/Getty Images **1** Photofest **2–3** Chayapon Bootboonneam /EyeEm/Getty Images **4–5** ABC/PhotoFest; Bettmann/Getty Images; Everett Collection; Photo 12/Alamy Stock Photo; Everett Collection; New World/Everett Collection; fjdelvalle/Getty Images; Everett Collection; TCD/Prod.DB/Alamy Stock Photo; DIMENSION FILMS /Album/Alamy Stock Photo; Lifestyle pictures/Alamy Stock Photo **6–7** Dan Foy (orangeacid)/Getty Images **8–9** Universal/Everett Collection; Everett Collection **10–11** Entertainment Pictures/Alamy Stock Photo **12–13** Niday Picture Library/Alamy Stock Photo; Andreea Alexandru/AP Images **14–15** Pictorial Parade/Getty Images; Moviestore Collection Ltd/Alamy Stock Photo; 20th Century Fox Film Corp/Everett Collection; Collection Christophel/Alamy Stock Photo **16–17** ABC/PhotoFest; Universal Pictures/Photofest; American International Pictures/Getty Images **18–19** Album/Alamy Stock Photo; PhotoFest; Album/Alamy Stock Photo; The Picture Art Collection/Alamy Stock Photo **20–21** AF archive/Alamy Stock Photo; Pictorial Press Ltd/Alamy Stock Photo; Metro-Goldwyn-Mayer (MGM)/Album/Alamy Stock Photo; AIP/PhotoFest **22–23** Moviestore Collection Ltd/Alamy Stock Photo; Warner Bros/PhotoFest.; Allstar Picture Library/Alamy Stock Photo; VIC PRODUCTIONS/Ronald Grant Archive/Alamy Stock Photo; Pictorial Press Ltd/Alamy Stock Photo **24–25** PhotoFest (2); AF archive/Alamy Stock Photo **26–27** UNIVERSAL PICTURES/Ronald Grant Archive/Alamy Stock Photo; Everett Collection **28–29** Bettmann/Getty Images **30–31** cineclassico/Alamy Stock Photo; PictureLux/The Hollywood Archive/Alamy Stock Photo; 20th Century Fox Film Corp./Everett Collection; Culture Club/Getty Images **32–33** Hulton Archive/Getty Images; COLUMBIA PICTURES/Ronald Grant Archive/Alamy Stock Photo; AF archive/Alamy Stock Photo **34–35** Everett Collection; WALT DISNEY PICTURES/Album/Alamy Stock Photo; Robbie Jack/Getty Images (2) **36–37** Universal/Everett Collection **38–39** VladGans/Getty Images; Universal/Everett Collection **40–41** Getty Images; Lanmas/Alamy Stock Photo; Historical image collection by Bildagentur-online/Alamy Stock Photo; Universal Pictures/PhotoFest **42–43** fjdelvalle/Getty Images; Universal Pictures/PhotoFest; Everett Collection **44–45** PictureLux/The Hollywood Archive/Alamy Stock Photo; Everett Collection; Photo 12/Alamy Stock Photo **46–47** Pictorial Press Ltd/Alamy Stock Photo; Pictorial Press Ltd/Alamy Stock Photo; PhotoFest; Patrick McMullan/Getty Images (2) **48–49** Warner Bros. Pictures/Everett Collection; Screen Gems/Everett Collection (2); Moviestore Collection Ltd/Alamy Stock Photo; Universal Pictures/Photofest **50–51** Allstar Picture Library Limited/Alamy Stock Photo; Moviestore Collection Ltd/Alamy Stock Photo **52–53** Moviestore Collection Ltd/Alamy Stock Photo **54–55** Warner Bros/PhotoFest; Hammer Films/PhotoFest; Everett Collection **56–57** Warner Brothers/Everett Collection; Atlaspix/Alamy Stock Photo; Brooke Palmer/Warner Bros. /Everett Collection; ScreenProd/Photononstop/Alamy Stock Photo; United Archives GmbH/Alamy Stock Photo **58–59** Pictorial Press Ltd/Alamy Stock Photo; Everett Collection **60–61** Courtesy of AMC **62–63** Photo 12/Alamy Stock Photo **64–65** United Archives GmbH/Alamy Stock Photo; Entertainment Pictures/Alamy Stock Photo; Allstar Picture Library Limited/Alamy Stock Photo **66–67** TCD/Prod.DB/Alamy Stock Photo; Moviestore Collection Ltd/Alamy Stock Photo; Sportsphoto/Alamy Stock Photo; Collection Christophel/Alamy Stock Photo; Everett Collection, Inc./Alamy Stock Photo **68–69** Rogue Pictures/Everett Collection (2); RGR Collection/Alamy Stock Photo **70–71** Courtesy of AMC (2); Paramount Pictures/PhotoFest **72–73** cineclassico/Alamy Stock Photo; Everett Collection; Weinstein Company/Everett Collection **74–75** Allstar Picture Library Limited/Alamy Stock Photo **76–77** PARAMOUNT PICTURES/Album/Alamy Stock Photo **78–79** 20th Century Fox Film Corp./Everett Collection; 20th Century Fox/PhotoFest; Everett Collection; MGM/Everett Collection **80–81** Michael Ochs Archives/Getty Images; TCD/Prod.DB/Alamy Stock Photo **82–83** Warner Brothers/Everett Collection; TCD/Prod.DB/Alamy Stock Photo; Moviestore Collection Ltd/Alamy Stock Photo; TCD/Prod.DB/Alamy Stock Photo **84–85** Bettmann/Getty Images; AP/Shutterstock; WikiMedia Commons; MGM/Everett Collection; AF archive/Alamy Stock Photo **86–87** Buena Vista Pictures/Everett Collection; John Baer/Universal Pictures/Everett Collection; TCD/Prod.DB/Alamy Stock Photo; Michael Tackett/Warner Bros. Pictures/Everett Collection; Photo 12/Alamy Stock Photo **88–89** Moviestore Collection Ltd/Alamy Stock Photo; 20the Century Fox/Henrey Fera/PhotoFest **90–91** TCD/Prod.DB/Alamy Stock Photo **92–93** Allied Artists Corporation/PhotoFest; Everett Collection; Allstar Picture Library Limited/Alamy Stock Photo; TCD/Prod.DB/Alamy Stock Photo; 20th Century Fox Film Corp/Everett Collection **94–95** Paramount Pictures/PhotoFest; Everett Collection, Inc./Alamy Stock Photo; Entertainment Pictures/Alamy Stock Photo; Photo 12/Alamy Stock Photo; Netflix /Everett Collection **96–97** Courtesy of 20th Century Fox; 20th Century Fox/Photofest (2) **98–99** Collection Christophel/Alamy Stock Photo; Everett Collection **100–101** Miramax/Everett Collection **102–103** Entertainment Pictures/Alamy Stock Photo; PhotoFest (2); New Line Features/PhotoFest **104–105** Collection Christophel/Alamy Stock Photo; LOBSTER ENTERPRISES/NIGHT/SEAN S. CUNNINGHAM FILMS/Album/Alamy Stock Photo **106–107** Lionsgate Films/PhotoFest; DIMENSION FILMS / Album/Alamy Stock Photo; AF archive/Alamy Stock Photo; PhotoFest; New Line Cinema/Everett Collection **108–109** Moviestore Collection Ltd/Alamy Stock Photo **110–111** Sony Pictures/Everett Collection; Bryanston Distributing Company/PhotoFest **112–113** Ronald Grant/GALATEA/Alamy Stock Photo; New Line Cinema/Everett Collection **114–115** WB/PhotoFest; ScreenProd/Photononstop/Alamy Stock Photo **116–117** Dimension Films/Everett Collection; Anchor Bay Entertainment/PhotoFest **118–119** FALCON INTERNATIONAL/Album/Alamy Stock Photo **120–121** Pictorial Press Ltd/Alamy Stock Photo; Everett Collection **122–123** 20th Century Fox/PhotoFest (3) **124–125** Universal Pictures/PhotoFest; Everett Collection (2); Photo 12/Alamy Stock Photo **126–127** Allstar Picture Library Limited/Alamy Stock Photo; Everett Collection (2) **128–129** Photo 12/Alamy Stock Photo; Dimension Films/ Everett Collection; Dimension Films/PhotoFest; Dimension Films/Everett Collection **130–131** Everett Collection (2); PhotoFest (2) **132–133** PhotoFest; Pictorial Press Ltd/Alamy Stock Photo; Universal Pictures/PhotoFest **134–135** AF archive/Alamy Stock Photo (2); Photo 12/Alamy Stock Photo **136–137** Photo 12/Alamy Stock Photo; Everett Collection, Inc./Alamy Stock Photo; Granamour Weems Collection/Alamy Stock Photo; MGM/UA/PhotoFest (2) **138–139** Universal Pictures/PhotoFest; Everett Collection (2) **140–141** Photo 12/Alamy Stock Photo; Everett Collection; Photo 12/Alamy Stock Photo **142–143** Everett Collection; World History Archive/Alamy Stock Photo; PhotoFest **144–145** SilverScreen/Alamy Stock Photo; AF archive/Alamy Stock Photo; ScreenProd/Photononstop/Alamy Stock Photo; Everett Collection **146–147** Pictorial Press Ltd/Alamy Stock Photo; Pictorial Press Ltd/Alamy Stock Photo; Compass International Pictures/